Whatever
Happened to
TANGANYIKA?

Whatever Happened to
TANGANYIKA?
THE PLACE NAMES THAT HISTORY LEFT BEHIND

HARRY CAMPBELL

PORTICO

First published in the United Kingdom in 2007 by
Portico Books
10 Southcombe Street
London
W14 0RA

An imprint of Anova Books Company Ltd

O9-10 BT 10.38

Illustrations by Annie McFadden

ISBN 9781906032050

09-10

A CIP catalogue record for this book is available from the British Library.

10 9 8 7 6 5 4 3 2 1

Typeset by SX Composing DTP, Rayleigh, Essex
Printed and bound by MPG Books Ltd, Bodmin, Cornwall

This book can be ordered direct from the publisher.
Contact the marketing department, but try your bookshop first.

www.anovabooks.com

TO THE MEMORY OF MY FATHER

Thanks to Emma Campbell for invaluable help in accessing research resources, to Ian Alexander for vital assistance with illustrations, to Alexander McCall Smith for his kindness and encouragement, and to Tom Bromley of Portico, a prince among publishers, for his unfailing patience and enthusiasm.

The locations, characters and events described in these pages are real – nearly all of them – and any similarity to actual places or persons, living or dead, is entirely intentional.

Far-called, our navies melt away;
On dune and headland sinks the fire:
Lo, all our pomp of yesterday
Is one with Nineveh and Tyre!

– Rudyard Kipling, 'Recessional' (1897)

What did Zimbabwe used to be called? – Rhodesia.
What did Iceland used to be called? – Bejam!

– Lynne Truss, *Eats, Shoots and Leaves* (2003)

Contents

Foreword

Place names have always fascinated me, especially those that with romantic associations. I remember the night I arrived at Casablanca Airport and got into an ancient taxi. As the headlights of the car swung round, they illuminated a road sign saying *Casablanca* – a strangely exciting moment for anyone who loves the film of that name. How many visitors have done that journey, perhaps in that very taxi, humming 'As Time Goes By?' Names are powerful triggers of memory and mood.

Time does indeed goes by, and some wonderful place names disappear. Tanganyika has gone, of course, as have so many other names of that era. As a boy I lived in Bulawayo, which was in Matabeleland, part of Southern Rhodesia. To the north, beyond the vanished Northern Rhodesia, was the Belgian Congo; to the south was the Bechuanaland Protectorate, which, before that, had been known as Khama's Country, on the edge of the Kalahari Desert. Bechuanaland, or BP as it was affectionately known, became Botswana and the Kalahari became the Kgaligadi; it was decided that it really was not a proper desert anyway, so 'Desert' went too. Some of the poetry went when these changes were made, even if new names, quite properly, may express more sensitively the aspirations of those who live there.

In this marvellous and intriguing book, Harry Campbell has achieved something that most scholars would give anything to achieve. He has created a whole new discipline – one which we may perhaps call *nostalgic geography*. Nostalgic geography reminds us of how things were and, very importantly, *where* they were. It might also sound a warning to over-enthusiastic name-changers: new names may not stick. So if any bureaucrats anywhere are casting eyes on Timbuktu, please desist.

Alexander McCall Smith
July 2007

Introduction

This little book is a tribute to the ghostly legions of places that have ceased to be. Places that are no longer called what they used to be called; names that have fallen by the wayside of history, or been deliberately cast aside. One moment you can't open a newspaper or switch on the television without hearing about Yugoslavia or Zaire, the next it's as if they had never existed. It is even possible that very young readers of these words may never have heard of such a place (though if this applies to you, stop chewing the cover and give the nice book back to Mummy or Daddy).

The maps change fast these days. If we dig out the family atlas, an item most people don't feel the need to replace very often, we will probably see names like Czechoslovakia or the USSR; those names disappeared only a few years ago, but how archaic the phrase 'Soviet Socialist Republic' sounds in the post-Cold War era. Meanwhile the name 'Congo', which perhaps had a slightly quaint and colonial ring a decade or so ago, is now right back in everyday use.[1]

Yes, a place name can date you. If you have heard of somewhere called Biafra, if you even know what continent it's on and what happened there, you were probably around in the 1960s when that name was a kind of synonym for the horrors of famine and civil war, and hearing it probably evokes the same shudder that later generations might get from names like Sarajevo, Rwanda or Darfur. But when did you last hear anyone refer to Biafra? Beirut, having spent the last twenty years or so waking up from the nightmare, recently reacquired for a while the hellish connotations it had in the 1980s. Another day, another name for the worst place on Earth.

[1] Actually, it never went away, since there are two countries named after that mighty African river.

Some of these places have disappeared off the map altogether, while others have simply been rebranded, as it were.[2] In recent times the reason for discarding an old name has often been the end of the colonial era. Sometimes the new name is about showing solidarity with a young nation whose attempt to break with the past is symbolised in a terminological makeover. Whichever, it can be hard to keep up and not worry about causing offence or looking ignorant. What are we supposed to call Bombay or Calcutta now, for example, especially if even the locals still seem to use the old name? Now that many British tourists go to Sevilla rather than Seville, or Thessaloniki rather than Salonica, will we soon be referring to Firenze and Moskva instead of Florence and Moscow? Is it still 'the Ukraine', or just 'Ukraine', and when exactly did Yugoslavia cease to exist? Is there, or is there not, a Somaliland at the moment as well as a Somalia?

It's not just 'Abroad' – confusion reigns at home too. British counties seem to change names and boundaries every generation or so, though people often carry on using the old names. Where is Dunbartonshire these days, and is there still a thing called Clackmannan? Wasn't Denbighshire done away with, and if so have they brought it back again, and what about poor old Rutland? Where or what was Salop and was it as dreary as it sounds?

'Hereford and Worcester' and 'Central Region' show how soulless names can be when they are coined by bureaucrats, but many old place names were exotic-sounding, evocative, almost poetic: Formosa, Bessarabia, Hispaniola, Muscat, Ragusa, Trebizond ... Wasn't it rather charming, idly thumbing through the atlas on a rainy day, dreaming of exotic holidays perhaps, to come across places like Pleasant Island or the Friendly Isles? And yet, a few of those names that sound like something from another era actually still exist: Brazzaville,

[2] To date, none of those mentioned has physically vanished, though the sad truth is that such will very probably be the fate of certain island nations when global warming takes its toll; in fact, it's already happening. Enjoy your independence while you can, Tuvalu and Tokelau, Kiribati and Kiritimati.

unlike Leopoldville, is more than just an exotic reference in the film *Casablanca*, and Blantyre is still Blantyre in Malawi just as in South Lanarkshire. And although many assume it to be as mythical as Ruritania or Atlantis, there actually is a Timbuktu.[3]

Getting it right is not always straightforward. After barely a generation under the name given it by Mobutu Sese Seko, Zaire is once more Congo, as it was in its days as the personal possession of Leopold II, King of the Belgians, and indeed for centuries before that. Constantinople and Leningrad have changed names more than once, and each name carries a different set of associations. Cities named after the likes of Ho Chi Minh and Karl Marx now seem like a short-lived political aberration. Even the headquarters of apartheid, Pretoria, is thinking of changing its name to something more, well, African. Some cities, like Rome and Calais, have changed not their spelling but their English pronunciation over the last century or three: it was 'Caliss', not 'Calay', that Mary Queen of Scots said would be found engraved on her heart when she died, and E M Forster's *A Room with a View* could be seen as a pun on the old pronunciation of the Italian capital.

Sometimes, as with Servia and Hindoostan, just a letter or two has changed, while other places are now known by a more local version of the name, like Beijing for Pekin(g) or the unrecognisable Chennai for Madras, leaving the anglicised version to fall into disuse. You would not be likely to ask for a ticket to Leghorn or Saragossa these days, even in English, but rather to Livorno or Zaragoza. Perhaps one day even the, shall we say, less culturally aware British visitor to Majorca ('ma-JAW-ka') will be calling the place Mallorca ('ma-YOR-ka') in deference to local convention.[4]

Names are political things, and using the old name, or rather refusing to change to the new one, can involve seeming to take sides: '. . . when I was out East you know, in Ceylon, or whatever they call it these days . . .' Should we strain for ever-

[3] It's in what we used to call French Sudan – but the word 'Sudan' has come to refer to a completely different part of Africa.
[4] Or perhaps not.

closer approximations to the local version, in order to show solidarity with the legitimate right to self-determination of a country such as, Moldova? Or should we wish the, er, Moldovans[5] well in their new-found independence, but stick to the established pattern and keep calling it Moldavia? After all, we don't feel the need to refer to Germany or Italy as Deutschland or Italia, when there are perfectly good English names for those countries.

But it's not just a matter of local modes versus foreign influence. Very often it's about knocking off his pedestal some hated representative of a former regime. Mostly this sort of official glorification is confined to the names of streets or buildings (and even that causes enough trouble when an old street sign or town plan still shows the old name), but at times it seems to have become a sort of patriotic sport. In the Soviet Union and its satellite states entire cities were often renamed, mostly after Stalin[6] and Lenin[7], and using the wrong name could get you into trouble. One writer on place names tells of a friend on a trip to Russia arriving in Kalinin and actually being arrested for using its pre-Soviet name, Tver.

This signalling of approval or disapproval through the choice of name exists at the highest levels, and can even be a matter of official foreign policy. For example, the United States government seems to feel that to call Burma by its new name, Myanmar, would be a sign of recognition of the repressive military regime currently running that country. The same name is often claimed by several parties: well over a decade after being admitted to the United Nations as a sovereign state, the 'Former Yugoslav Republic of Macedonia' still officially goes by that cumbersome, determinedly neutral title. It may be a mouthful but it's necessary if business is not

---

[5] Moldovese?? Moldovs???

[6] You know the kind of thing: Stalingrad, Stalinogród, Stalinabad, Stalinstadt, Stalinogorsk, Stalinsk, Sztálinváros, Staliniri, Stalino, Qyteti Stalin (Stalin City) or just Stalin.

[7] Leningrad, Leninabad, Leninkent, Leninogorsk, Leninsk, Leninsky, Leninskoye, Leninváros, Leningori, Lenino, Lenin, you get the idea.

to be disrupted by terminological disputes over the contentious name of Macedonia.

Why do British cities seem to change their names less often than those of some countries? One reason must be the relative political stability that we in the UK have been blessed with in recent times. Of course places do have different names in the different languages that have been around at various times – Celtic, Pictish, Latin, Norse, Anglo-Saxon – but as for names used in English, generally they are much as they were in the famous Domesday Book of 1086, always allowing for the fact that the language itself has changed a bit in the last thousand years or so. British name-changes have tended to be a matter of territorial reshuffles for the sake of administrative efficiency, rather than the expunging of a political undesirable or the ousting of a hated oppressor – though perhaps the Welsh nationalists who defaced monolingual English road signs in the 1970s might not agree about that, nor the warring factions of Northern Ireland, nor even the fervent defenders of the absurdly tiny county of Rutland.

However, many people carry on using the old county names almost as if, well, perish the thought, but as if they somehow just didn't care much about the wonderful efficiencies supposedly to be gained by restructuring local government services on a more logical geographical basis. In the case of Wales the 'new' (in fact, medieval) names like Gwynedd, Dyfed and Powys, which replaced the 'old' shires (Flintshire, Caernarvonshire and so on) in the 1970s did seem to catch on straight away, but for some reason in Scotland the pre-70s counties like Lanarkshire and Dumfriesshire refused to go away, and have since gone on to survive yet another reorganisation. The police force covering much of the West of Scotland still calls itself after Strathclyde, the ancient kingdom which, reinvented in the 1970s, had scarcely achieved the age of majority before ceasing to exist for governmental purposes in 1996.

And why not? After all, county names belong to the people, not just to local government officials. They are more than units of territory or administrative areas; they have history and associations that go back a long way and run surprisingly deep – as the bureaucrats probably found out when they rode roughshod over traditional rivalries and rolled together the counties of Hereford and Worcester.[8]

Perhaps, along with our supposed sense of political moderation and fair play, there's a kind of British reserve, or even just inertia, that prevents us renaming cities with the cavalier abandon we show towards counties. Otherwise, would we have had Oliverstowns and Cromwellvilles springing up during the Civil War? Would London be known as Parliament City? It's not that we refuse to commemorate people in place names: there are states, mountains, islands, lakes and streets galore named in honour of British monarchs, and extraterrestrial bodies called after all sorts of people. Brand-new settlements such as colonial outposts (Kimberley, Ladysmith) and garrison towns (Fort William, Fort Augustus) do often bear the name of their founder or patron, and of course Cecil Rhodes had a whole country named after him — not bad for a parson's son from Bishop's Stortford. Rhodesia had to go, but if those Forts can survive un-renamed despite the Scottish hatred of the 'butcher' Duke of Cumberland they immortalise, there's every hope for the new towns commemorating Thomas Telford the engineer, Peter Lee the trade unionist and even Viscount Craigavon, first Prime Minister of Northern Ireland.

So, it's rather more complicated than a simple list of names 'before and after': there are some stories to tell. Welcome to the Museum of Dead Place Names. Let's open that out-of-date atlas and start browsing. Where do all the old names go to die? Or, as a friend of mine once wondered aloud, 'Whatever happened to Tanganyika?'[9]

---

[8] Apparently they turned down an imaginative suggestion to call the new county 'Wyvern', after the Rivers Wye and Severn, rather than the mythical two-legged dragon.

[9] Thanks for the title, Ian.

Pleasant Island

Pleasant Island, or the Republic of Nauru as we know it today, must surely be one of the most unusual countries in the world, and perhaps also one of the most unfortunate. It's one of the world's smallest sovereign states, both in terms of land area[10] and population,[11] and supposedly the only one without an official capital.[12] If you're ever at a loose end for a few weeks in the South Pacific, or perhaps just flicking through an old atlas one evening, you'll find the erstwhile Pleasant Island about two and a half thousand miles north of Australia and about the same distance southwest of Hawaii, at 0°32′ S, 166°55′ E. If you'd rather check someone's in before you set off, the international dialling code is 674.

The ancient kingdom of Nauru was given the name Pleasant Island in 1798 by one Captain John Fearn, master of the British whaling ship *Hunter*, who called by en route from New Zealand to the China Seas, and obviously liked the look of the place. The territory was annexed by Germany in 1888 as part of German New Guinea. After the First World War, when Germany lost so many of its overseas possessions, it became a League of Nations (later United Nations) Mandate territory administered jointly by Britain, Australia and New Zealand.

But why would anyone care enough to take over this tiny coral atoll, lost in the vastness of the Pacific? In a word, guano. Bird droppings, if you prefer. The fortune of this little lump of rock, and perhaps ultimately its curse, is that for millions of years it was, basically, a toilet for seabirds. The value of these

[10] About eight square miles.
[11] Perhaps twelve thousand, though nobody seems to know exactly.
[12] The 18-member parliament meets near Nauru International Airport, just next to the police station.

accumulated deposits became clear at the beginning of the twentieth century with the booming demand for 'super-phosphate', the basis of artificial fertilisers. Unfortunately, guano was more or less the island's only natural resource, and a more or less finite one. The 'topside', as it's known to the locals, is now a pitted moonscape of coral outcrops from around which the precious phosphate has been comprehensively mined out. The colonial powers used up this poor little country and spat it out. Sad to say, Pleasant Island is probably not the name that would spring to mind today.

Where do you go to find an income when 90 per cent of your country has been reduced to an unproductive, uninhabitable wasteland, when just to keep your population alive you have to import food and even drinking water from thousands of miles away? Even then you'll have problems bringing your hard-won supplies

ashore, since the island is surrounded by a coral reef and has no proper harbour.

By the time the island achieved independence in 1968, the phosphates were already about to run out, and although they gave Nauruans one of the highest per-capita incomes in the world,[13] that income was unwisely invested in various unlikely

[13] This was very much a mixed blessing, since the money brought with it all the ills that flesh is heir to: complacency, lack of aspiration, educational underachievement, an unhealthy diet of high-calorie imported food and consequent diabetes rates among the worst to be found anywhere. In a country with one of the world's highest population densities, where agriculture is a thing of the past, and which lies thousands of miles from the nearest arable land, fresh fruit and vegetables are almost unknown and tinned

and unsuccessful projects. The islanders went into real estate, buying office blocks and hotels in Australia and Hawaii. Their flagship tower block, Nauru House in Melbourne, developed something called 'concrete cancer', which eats away at the structure of the building. Now it has been sold to pay off creditors. A brand-new hotel was built in the Marshall Islands but never even opened.

Elements of tragicomedy crept in. Perhaps fittingly for a nation in the South Pacific, Nauru decided to put money into West End musical theatre – it became an 'angel', to the tune of 3.9 million Australian dollars. The islanders had never seen a musical, but the stardust evidently worked its magic and they backed a show about the life of Leonardo da Vinci. It was called (what else) *Leonardo*, and it ran for less than a week.

In the 1990s, as desperation set in, Nauru started marketing itself as a tax haven, attracting considerable sums from blue-chinned business gentlemen from Eastern Europe who wanted to set up a bank but were too busy to keep records. Suddenly it was home to some 400 banks, none of which had any physical presence on the island. Not surprisingly, this got Nauru into very hot water with international anti-money-laundering agencies and did the prospects of foreign aid no good at all. Another dead end.

In 2001 Nauru took in a shipload of refugees who had been denied permission to dock in Australia. Could the island have a future as a detention centre for asylum seekers and prisoners of the so-called 'war on terror'? But the costs of servicing such a remote settlement would be astronomical, and any thoughts

bully beef with rice becomes the staple diet. Even road deaths rocketed, now that everyone could afford a sports car – this in a place that only has two roads and one junction. Meanwhile Air Nauru flew empty planes to unprofitable destinations and sometimes cancelled services to run errands for the President. This is the so-called 'resource curse' that afflicts small places with only one valuable resource and one chance to get it right; it means that your country's wealth can actually inhibit, rather than promote, economic growth and wellbeing.

of turning it into Australia's Guantanamo Bay have been abandoned.

Then, or so it has been alleged, Nauru became embroiled in 'Operation Weasel', a bizarre plot to smuggle North Korean defectors to the West through Nauruan puppet embassies in China and the USA. In 2005 Air Nauru's only remaining plane was impounded by the Export–Import Bank of the United States in lieu of unpaid loan repayments. But the hardest blow of all may come from an even more powerful force than the American money-men. For an island rising no more than 70 metres above sea level, where only the coastline is habitable, global warming is a very real threat.

Pity the island micro-nation with no natural resources left, a major diabetes problem caused by excessive consumption of unhealthy Western food and too much driving round in luxury cars, unreliable relations with the West, an encroaching sea-line, and nowhere to turn to build a sustainable future. You can't make a fortune out of exotic stamps. Even Nauru's Internet domain name, '.nr', doesn't turn out to be a windfall like Tuvalu's '.tv', or Tonga's '.to'.[14] It's tempting to think that Nauru is all washed up and on the rocks. But that would be too sad a line for even the cheesiest of musicals.

[14] And why is that valuable? Well, it means you can sell people internet addresses like 'www.come.to/. . .' and 'www.how.to/. . .'.

Burma

But Burma still exists, you say? That's true as far as many authorities are concerned, the government of the United States among them. When we hear the 'new' name, Myanmar, it is often quoted alongside the old one, rather as Derry and Londonderry come bolted together in polite society and the name 'Macedonia' must be preceded by the words 'Former Yugoslav Republic of' so as to avoid offence in certain quarters. We're familiar with the idea of names reverting to pre-colonial ones, or changing to something closer to the local term. But how did Burma, not an obviously European-sounding name like Rhodesia or Leopoldville, come to be morphed into the seemingly unconnected Myanmar?

As with many South Asian languages, concepts of formality are deeply ingrained in Burmese. The everyday colloquial name of the country is *Bama*, perhaps recognisable as the origin of 'Burma'. *Myanma* is the literary word for the same country, and Bama (hence Burma) may well have developed from that name, though the etymology and original literal meaning are unclear. So if they are both good Burmese words, if it's not a matter of throwing off the yoke of linguistic imperialism, why the change?

Burma is a complex country, and its name has long been a matter of political controversy. The dominant group, the Burmans, are only one of many ethnicities. In 1886 Britain annexed this historically warlike and politically unstable region to its Indian Empire, and set up the Anglo-Burma Oil Company. *The Times* opined in 1911 that 'few companies in the history of British commerce have yielded such magnificent dividends', but of course those dividends did not stay in Burma. Opposition to the British ran high, and the outbreak of war in 1939 seemed to provide an opportunity to shake off the yoke.

But promises of independence made by the Japanese when they took over the country in 1942 came to nothing, and Burma soon found itself under British administration once again. It was a time of violence and turmoil, and independence in 1948 failed to bring much stability. To cut a very long story short, insurgencies by Muslims, Communists and Socialists of all hues were followed by military coups in 1962 and 1988, since when international economic pressure and anti-government demonstrations have done little to break the stranglehold of the military dictatorship known (until recently) by the sinister-sounding acronym of SLORC, the State Law and Order Restoration Council.

In 1989 SLORC decided to review the official English translations of Burmese place names, and decreed that Myanmar should replace Burma. Aside from the aim of bringing English names closer to Burmese pronunciation, it is claimed officially that Myanma is more inclusive of the ethnic minorities of the Union of Burma, of which the ethnic Bama are only a part, though opponents allege that in fact the 'new' name Myanmar is felt as even more foreign by the non-Burmese-speaking minorities on whom it has been imposed. In a sense a colonial name can be felt less divisive within an ethnically diverse country than a local name, in the same way that colonial languages like English and French have stayed on as the educated lingua franca throughout so much of the developing world. It is even alleged that there is an element of official repression in the name itself, since the junta's distrust of the people is so great that colloquial language forms are perceived as a threat to authority.

So the name Myanmar has not been widely adopted, since the current regime has more or less no international recognition, having after all annulled the free and fair elections of 1990 and kept the rightful prime minister, Aung San Suu Kyi, under house arrest ever since.

On a more trivial level, quite apart from the uncertainty

most people feel about how to pronounce the new name, abandoning the old one would break the link with such commercial legends as the American company Burma-Vita. Their shaving cream Burma-Shave, whose ingredients claimed some sort of connection with Burma for the sake of exotic chic, was famous for its playful roadside adverts, spread out over six sequential billboards, which were a feature of the American highway from the 1920s to the 1960s. Some of them are nicely crafted pieces of folk verse:

> DOES YOUR HUSBAND
> MISBEHAVE
> GRUNT AND GRUMBLE
> RANT AND RAVE?
> SHOOT THE BRUTE SOME
> BURMA-SHAVE

Often they played on the theme of success with the opposite sex, or lack of it:

> A CHIN
> WHERE BARBED WIRE
> BRISTLES STAND
> IS BOUND TO BE
> A NO MA'AMS LAND
> BURMA-SHAVE

Many took the form of road-safety messages:

> DON'T LOSE
> YOUR HEAD
> TO GAIN A MINUTE
> YOU NEED YOUR HEAD
> YOUR BRAINS ARE IN IT
> BURMA-SHAVE

A Burma is also, according to the *Oxford English*

Dictionary, 'a kind of cheroot manufactured in Burma and with a peculiar aroma'. That's 'peculiar' as in distinctive, of course, rather than odd.[15]

---

[15] Or perhaps not.

Rutland

Rutland. Sometimes a word is just right. If you had to invent the name of this almost mythical English county, this land of lost content, you couldn't do much better. It would surely contain places called Oakham and Uppingham and Barley-thorpe and Nether Hambleton – and it does. It belongs with Adlestrop and Blandford Forum and suchlike icons of the vanished bucolic idyll that was England, oh, any time when the writer was young and happy. The antithesis of Slough.

A nineteenth-century source claims that the name comes from the red earth (ruddle or reddle) used for marking the fleeces of sheep – a suitably picturesque if inaccurate derivation. Be that as it may, people have loved the name enough to export it widely. There are Rutlands in Illinois, Iowa, Massachusetts, Michigan, Minnesota, New York, Ohio, Pennsylvania, Vermont, Wisconsin and both Dakotas. Appro-priately enough, almost none of these places can boast a population into four figures, though the largest, Rutland Massachusetts, was once one of the world's leading producers of marble. Henry David Thoreau said he would rather look toward it than toward Jerusalem. There are at least two Rutland Islands: one a tiny speck of rock in the Bay of Bengal, part of the Andaman Islands, and another off the coast of Donegal, named in honour of Charles Manners, Fourth Duke of Rutland, one-time Lord Lieutenant of Ireland.

Rutlandshire was famously England's smallest county, less than twenty miles in each direction, smaller in population than anywhere but the City of London[16] and rising no higher above

[16] The famous Square Mile, London's financial district, may have a daytime population of some 311,000 workers, but fewer than 10,000 people live there.

sea level than 646 feet. It lay modestly tucked in between the equally unassuming shires of Leicester, Lincoln and Northampton. Mentioned in the Domesday Book, naturally, Rutland was recognised as a county as far back as the twelfth century. Seven hundred years later it was divided into the hundreds of Oakham, Alstoe, Martinsley, Wrandike and East. The Rutlandese must have been cautiously optimistic. The Lord of the Manor of Oakham even felt confident enough to levy a tax on every monarch and peer of the realm passing through – one horseshoe. They put them up on the walls of the twelfth-century Oakham Castle, where an impressive collection has built up over the centuries.

Then, disaster. Poor Rutland vanished without trace in the local government reorganisation of 1974, merged with Leicestershire in the teeth of popular opposition.

Of course this was not the first time the land of the red sheep dye had been under threat. Even in the aftermath of world war, it had not escaped notice that a county of barely 20,000 souls was not a practical proposition in the twentieth century when, according to the 1948 Boundary Commission, ten times that number was a sensible size. But the fighting blood of Rutland was up, and a petition was signed by three out of four inhabitants.

Again in 1960 the abolitionist hordes were beating at the gates; again, the Men of Rutland did not cease from mental fight, nor did their pens sleep in their hands, and after a four-year battle of attrition the Save Rutland Campaign gained the day – give or take the loss to Cambridgeshire of the Isle of Ely, and the annexing by cruel Huntingdon of something called the Soke of Peterborough.

In 1974, however, Rutland's luck ran out. Another fragment of Olde English quaintness swept away in the tide of Progress. A divisional dodo, a quagga among counties. RIP.

But as they'll no doubt tell you in Oakham, Alstoe, Martinsley, Wrandike and the less imaginatively named East, what goes around comes around, and in the re-reorganisation of 1997, the Soke of Peterborough was avenged: Rutland was restored to life as a unitary authority.[17]

So how can the *Encyclopaedia Britannica* tell us so dismissively that 'the county played little subsequent role in English history'? Has it never heard of Rutland morocco, that fine roan leather used in the bookbinding trade? And what about Rutland Water? – not one of those trendy bottled elixirs, but Britain's largest reservoir, a breeding site for the osprey, the rare bird of prey you thought was confined to Scotland. Better not underestimate this tiny but resilient little county, which after living quietly for eight or nine centuries and suffering death by bureaucrat, has come back from the grave to host endangered fish-eating raptors. History is a long time, and it ain't over yet.

[17] It has therefore, strictly speaking, no place in this book, though if what goes around really does come around we must surely be due a re-re-reorganisation soon.

Illyria

What country, friends, is this?
This is Illyria, lady.

Not an American tourist on a whistle-stop tour, nor a sleep-deprived backpacker losing track of geography: that was Shakespeare's shipwrecked heroine Viola and the sea-captain in *Twelfth Night*. And well might she ask. What or where was the mellifluous-sounding 'Illyria', exactly?

Jean-Paul Sartre used the name as the setting of his play *Les Mains Sales*, in which Illyria is a fictional East European country, presumably based upon Hungary, about to be annexed to the Eastern Bloc at the end of the Second World War. Like the Forest of Arden, Illyria is actually a real place that has taken on the flavour of a semi-mythical other world. The real-life Illyria was the Roman province of Illyricum on the east coast of the Adriatic, running south from what is now Austria and Slovenia in the north, taking in Fiume (now called Rijeka) and Ragusa (Dubrovnik as we know it today), all the way down the coast of Croatia and Albania.

In fact, Illyria is sometimes equated with Albania, at least in the sense that the Albanians are considered by some to be the descendants of the ancient Illyrian people. Their language may, though this is controversial, be related to the extinct Illyrian tongues, of which only a handful of words have come down to us. Incidentally, if the ancient historian Arrian of Nicomedia (Lucius Flavius Arrianus) is to be believed, the Illyrians indulged in human sacrifice, but though rural Albania can certainly be a violent place, they don't do that any more.

The classical Illyria was divided into Pannonia in the north and Dalmatia in the south. Dalmatia is probably named after a tribe called the *Delmatae*, who in turn may possibly have something to do with sheep (*delmë* in Albanian). It gave its name to an ecclesiastical garment called the dalmatic, a kind of long wide-sleeved tunic derived from the ancient Byzantine *dalmatica*.

Dalmatia also had its own language, though nothing to do with Illyrian; Dalmatian was a Latin-based language spoken in various towns along the coast. One of its dialects managed to survive into the nineteenth century.

Of course, this is just teasing. The first sort of Dalmatian anyone thinks of is the spotted dogs so prized by Cruella de Vil, traditionally used as running-dogs to accompany and guard the coaches of the rich. And if you're wondering why Dalmatians are called

Dalmatians, it's bad news: no one really knows.

The name Illyria was revived in the nineteenth century by Napoleon, whose empire included the 'Illyrian Provinces' from 1809 to 1813. They were given to Austria by the Congress of Vienna and reconstituted, without Dalmatia, as the Kingdom of Illyria, which survived until 1849. But to find your way to Illyria today you would need a time machine rather than a ship.[18]

[18] Or at least a spaceship, since there is an asteroid named after Illyria. It was discovered in 1929 by the German astronomer Karl Wilhelm Reinmuth, who found nearly 400 of the things, naming many of them after classical people and places. So on that basis you could also visit Viola, or even travel to Atlantis if you felt like it.

Guinea

Is there a place called Guinea these days, or not? In fact, aren't there several? It's one of those questions you might need to scratch your head over for a moment, since Guinea is surely one of the world's more over-used and confusing place names. The French, Spanish and Portuguese each had a colonial territory of that name. Today there are no fewer than four countries with the name Guinea.

Guinea, *tout court*, refers by default to the old French Guinea in West Africa, now the Republic of Guinea (*République de Guinée*). On its northern border we find the smaller country that from 1446 to 1974 was Portuguese Guinea, and before that the kingdom of Gabù in the medieval Manding Empire of Mali; it's now known as Guinea-Bissau (*República da Guiné-Bissau*). Even smaller, about 10,000 square miles in area, perhaps 500 miles further south and a long way east, is Equatorial Guinea, made up of Río Muni and the islands of Bioko (previously Fernando Pó) and Annobón. And the fourth Guinea? If the last one fails to come to mind that may be because it's in a different part of the world altogether: New Guinea of course, in the Pacific Ocean, the world's second largest island, after Greenland.

The name Guinea came into English from Portuguese, but its ultimate origin is not clear, though some derive it from a Berber word or phrase meaning 'land of the black men'. Like many African place names, such as Sudan, Congo and Biafra, it has been used very vaguely over the centuries to refer to indeterminate areas of West Africa, and even more vaguely to anything somehow a bit exotic. The guinea fowl is from Africa, yes, but why are guinea pigs called guinea pigs when they are not pigs and not from Guinea but South America? No one really knows, though the *Oxford English Dictionary* suggests it may be through some perceived resemblance to the guinea hog, which actually is a species of pig. However, guinea pig is apparently an older term than guinea hog. 'Confusion with Guiana,'[19] the dictionary reassures us, 'seems unlikely.'

Many of the associations are not so cuddly. In American English 'guinea', sometimes spelled guinny or ginny, is an old insult for an immigrant of Mediterranean origin. A Guinea merchant or Guinea-man was one who traded with Guinea, but by extension a slave-trader. The West African associations of gold and slaves[20] come together in the word Guinea. Joseph Spence, a professor of poetry and modern history at Oxford in the early eighteenth century, retails in his *Anecdotes,*

Observations and Characters of Books and Men the following put-down: 'I don't know how great you may be, (said the Guinea-man), but I don't like your looks: I have often bought a man, much better than both of you together, all muscles and bones, for ten guineas.'

Older readers may remember guineas. At one time professional services were charged in guineas, and things like racehorses and works of art still seem to be. A guinea is 21 shillings, or £1.05 in decimal coinage, though until 1717 the

[19] Guyana as we spell it nowadays, since independence from Britain in 1966.
[20] There was a Coast named after each, after all.

value fluctuated according to the market value of the gold the coins were made of, and the very first guinea coins struck in 1663, 'in the name and for the use of the Company of Royal Adventurers of England trading with Africa', were worth 20 shillings. To maintain the African theme, they each bore a little picture of an elephant. Guineas have not been minted since 1813, but a memory of the word lingers on in Egyptian Arabic, referring to the Egyptian pound: al-Gunaih.

Guinea worm is the common term for a very nasty parasite indeed, a nematode or roundworm that lives in water fleas and enters the bodies of humans and animals though contact with stagnant water. It has been known about for thousands of years and has even been found preserved in Egyptian mummies. Its Latin name, *Dracunculus medinensis*, means 'the little dragon of Medina', and in parts of Africa where dracunculiasis has not quite been eradicated it is still often dealt with by the age-old method of gently extracting the worm, through the ulcer it creates, by winding it round a piece of stick like a reel of cotton. Because of this it is thought by some to be the origin of the ancient symbol of medicine, the caduceus: a staff with a serpent coiled around it, which might or might not remind you of the results of a nematode extraction.[21]

---

[21] Readers please note that the foregoing factoid is strictly for entertainment purposes only and no guarantees of any sort are offered as to its accuracy.

Hispaniola

When in 1492 Columbus sailed the ocean blue he ended up running aground on the second largest island in the Caribbean. He called it simply Spanish Island – *la Isla Española* – which came into English as Hispaniola. It was also known to Europeans as Santo Domingo, San Domingo or Saint-Domingue, after Saint Dominic, founder of the Dominican Order. The native population knew it as *Quisqueya* or *Ayti* ('land of mountains'), and this is where we get another name for the place: Haiti, or Hayti as it used to be spelled in English.

The modern state of Haiti occupies only the western third of the island, which was ceded by the Spanish to the French in 1697. The rest is now the Dominican Republic,[22] and the name Santo Domingo now applies to its capital, the descendant of a city founded by Columbus's brother Bartholomew in 1496 on the east bank of the River Ozama. It was named Nueva Isabela after Queen Isabel of Aragon and Castile, and it was the capital of the first Spanish colony in the New World. It was destroyed by a hurricane in 1502 and rebuilt on the other side of the river. When another hurricane struck in 1930, the city was rebuilt by Rafael Leónidas Trujillo Molina (who had just been elected president) and renamed Ciudad Trujillo in 1936. It's usually a bad sign when presidents start renaming things after themselves, and sure enough Trujillo soon awarded himself the title of Generalissimo[23] and stopped bothering with elections. An assassin's bullet ended his brutal, racist and

[22] Not be confused with the Commonwealth of Dominica (stress on the third syllable) about 500 miles away in the Lesser Antilles, supposedly 'discovered' on Sunday, the Lord's Day, *domingo* in Spanish.
[23] He was less officially known as the Goat (*el Chivo*) because of his prodigious sexual appetites.

profiteering dictatorship in 1961, and Trujillo City reverted to Santo Domingo.

Of course Haiti has seen even worse things under the notorious François 'Papa Doc' Duvalier and his machete-wielding thugs, the Tonton Macoutes; the death toll of his reign of terror is counted in tens of thousands. Having been elected democratically, he went on to declare himself President-for-Life[24] and on his death in 1971 was succeeded by his son Jean-Claude, nicknamed 'Baby Doc'. At nineteen years old he was the youngest president of any nation in the world and no doubt the least competent.[25]

It was not until 1986 that democratic leadership returned to this traumatised country under Jean-Bertrand Aristide. Political stability seems as elusive as ever, though, and what was the richest colony in the western hemisphere is now said to be its poorest state. Literacy rates are well below 50 per cent and average income is just one quarter of that of its next-door neighbour, the Dominican Republic. Haiti is classified by the UN as a Least Developed Country, part of what is informally known as the Fourth World.

But two centuries ago Haiti saw what was perhaps its finest hour. To set the scene, when Columbus had arrived on Hispaniola it was populated by the Arawak or more specifically Taíno people, Amerindians thought to have migrated from South America. To them we owe the hammock and the barbecue[26] and words like hurricane, canoe, tobacco, mahogany and maize. They were said to be a peaceful people, harassed by the more aggressive Caribs, whose name gives us the word cannibal. But neither group survived the arrival of the

[24] Not to mention Unquestioned Leader of the Revolution, Apostle of National Unity, Worthy Heir of the Founders of the Haitian Nation, Restorer of the Fatherland, Chief of the National Community and, as if that wasn't enough to keep any dictator busy, Zacharias, the Great Electrifier of Souls.

[25] Having spent money like water while his people starved, he was eventually forced into luxurious exile in France, though rumour has it his ex-wife has since taken him to the cleaners.

[26] Which originally meant a wooden framework for sleeping on, as well as for smoking or grilling meat.

Europeans: those who did not die of smallpox were soon worked to death.

What we now call Caribbeans are the descendants of Africans brought over in their thousands as slaves to harvest sugar cane. In French colonial times there were various distinct sectors of society: the *petits Blancs* (poor whites such as labourers, slave dealers and shopkeepers), the *grands blancs* (plantation owners, usually minor aristocrats or upwardly mobile bourgeois), the *gens de couleur* (free blacks or mixed-race 'mulattoes') and slaves. Their living conditions were such that having children was more or less impossible, and their numbers were continually replenished from Africa. In this deeply divided society the wealth was owned by a small, decadent and racist elite, and the economy powered by vast numbers of downtrodden human chattels – around half a million of them,[27] representing about half of all the slaves in the Caribbean.

With the French Revolution of 1789 sending ripples around the empire, conditions were ripe for rebellion, and in 1791 the slaves of Haiti rose up. Their greatest leader was a domestic slave who went by the splendid name of François-Dominique[28] Toussaint Louverture.[29] The result, to cut a long story very short, was that Haiti's slaves were freed in 1793 and Louverture appointed Governor-General by the revolutionary government of France. He expelled the British and French and took control of the whole island in 1801 under his own constitution – an extraordinary achievement. As the American abolitionist Wendell Phillips pointed out, 'Napoleon was

[27] The ratio of slaves to *gens de couleur* remains much the same as that of black to mixed-race Haitians today.

[28] Or Pierre-Dominique.

[29] So called supposedly because he was born on All Saints' Day (*le Toussaint*) and, according to the story, because as a military commander he could always find a way through: '*Cet homme fait l'ouverture partout!*' In a lighter moment we might recall other splendidly named Haitians such as Joseph-Balthazar Inginac, Jean-Baptiste Pointe du Sable, Charlemagne-Masséna Péralte and Aubelin Jolicoeur, supposedly immortalised by Graham Greene as Petit Pierre in *The Comedians*.

educated from a boy in the best military schools in Europe [and] at the age of 27 was placed at the head of the best troops Europe ever saw', while Toussaint Louverture 'never saw a soldier till he was fifty'.

When Napoleon's forces tried to regain control and reintroduce slavery, Louverture resisted and held them to a treaty under which slavery was prohibited. But the French still suspected him of plotting an uprising; he was arrested and taken to France for interrogation. He died in prison of pneumonia in 1803, but is revered to this day as a visionary leader and a remarkable man who cared for the wellbeing of all races. He led the only successful slave rebellion in modern history and was the architect of the world's first independent black state. Wordsworth eulogised him thus:

> There's not a breathing of the common wind
> That will forget thee; thou hast great allies;
> Thy friends are exultations, agonies,
> And love, and man's unconquerable mind.

Halicarnassus

It may sound more like an obscure anatomical term, perhaps a small and unimportant bone in the hand, but Halicarnassus was a very major place in its day. Its history goes back thousands of years, and it was the birthplace of Herodotus, the 'father of history' himself, in 484 BC. In classical times it was the capital of the satrapy of Caria. One satrap[30] was laid to rest in a tomb there so impressive that it was ranked as one of the Seven Wonders of the ancient world, and even entered the English language. He was Mausolus, and his resting place was the original Mausoleum.

Halicarnassus, known in the Middle Ages as Petronium, is in what is now Turkey. Its archaeological riches are too many and glorious to describe here, but it is better known today as a major beach resort specialising in sun, sea, sand and, well, all the carnal pleasures. The modern-day name for it is Bodrum, but if the stories are to be believed, the Romeos in the union-jack boxer shorts prefer to call it 'Bedroom'.

---

[30] A provincial governor in the Persian empire.

Neutral Moresnet

It's very straightforward for us Brits. Borders are a rather foreign concept; by and large the country stops where the land stops and the sea begins. Invasion may have been a recurrent fear until recently, but (give or take a few little local incidents) it hasn't actually happened properly for the best part of a thousand years. This is quite something, when you consider that most parts of Europe have been fought over at frequent intervals, often being passed back and forth between rival powers, so that one person could have several nationalities in one lifetime without even moving from the village they were born in. In the colossal geopolitical struggle, we petty men creep about, keeping our heads down and getting on with life. Meanwhile, as the superpowers lock antlers and take up the strain, as the tectonic plates of history grind past each other, little slivers and shards tend to break away and splinter off. Very little ones indeed, sometimes.

Think of the tiniest, most absurd microstate you can imagine. Forget Liechtenstein and Monaco, even Vatican City; did you know that for a century or so there existed a tiny scrap of territory about three miles long, less than 1,000 acres in area, known as Neutral Moresnet? Where else would it be but next to mighty Belgium, that complex little country riven with conflicting minorities, where a whole government can be brought down by a dispute over the language rights of a municipality of six villages?[31] While not exactly a sovereign state, it was a neutral territory in the sense that it belonged wholly to no one country, being jointly governed by on the one hand Prussia, and on the other Holland and then Belgium.

[31] The Voeren or Fourons, but that's for another book.

The modern states of Germany, Belgium and the Netherlands meet at a place called Vaalserberg, the Vaals 'mountain', which at 1,000 feet above sea level is the highest point in the Netherlands. There, at the so-called *Parc des Trois Frontières* or *Drielandenpunt* ('Three Countries Point'), you can stand with one foot in each of them. Or at least you could if you had three feet, unlike the average person who is equipped with, statistically speaking, slightly fewer than two. But this is no place for frivolity. A moment of silence, please. You are standing at the northern extreme of what was Neutral Moresnet.[32]

Why was this tiny scrap of land fought over so bitterly by two of the great powers of the day, at the Congress of Vienna in 1815 and for a century thereafter? The answer lies in the soil. Since prehistory, naturally occurring ores of zinc had been melted together with copper to produce brass, but pure zinc was only synthesised at the beginning of the nineteenth century, by a chemist from Liège, Jean-Jacques-Daniel Dony (1759–1819). In 1806 the Napoleonic authorities granted him a concession at a place called Altenberg or Vieille Montagne, just north of the main road that runs between the Belgian city of Liège to the southwest and Aachen (Aix-la-Chapelle if you prefer) just a few miles away in Germany. It's also known by the name of the commodity

---

[32] So in those days you would have needed four legs.

itself: Kelmis in Dutch or La Calamine in French.[33] As in calamine lotion.

Holland and Prussia could not come to an agreement on this desirable asset, and so as an interim measure agreed to treat the district (*mairie*) of Moresnet like ancient Gaul: they divided it into three parts. Moresnet village became part of the Kingdom of the Netherlands, New Moresnet went to Prussia, and the bit in between became a neutral territory under the joint administration ('condominium') of both powers. In 1830 the Dutch zone became part of the new country of Belgium, but Neutral Moresnet remained doggedly neutral, its affairs handled by a mayor and ten-member council appointed by Royal Commissioners representing the Prussian monarchy and the King of the Belgians.

And all this was still temporary, in theory, as no one had been able to agree who the territory should finally be ceded to. But meanwhile life was good in Neutral Moresnet, by all accounts. Being a stateless individual with no proper nationality can be inconvenient, but there are advantages too: low taxes, low prices, no import tariffs, the right to make home-brewed spirits for home consumption – and the chance to export it quietly across the border when no one's looking. And since your true-born, dinkie-die Neutral Moresnetians, descended from the original 1815 inhabitants, had neither Belgian nor Prussian citizenship, these 'indigenous sons of the soil' as *The Times* called them in 1903 could not be called up for military service by either power. In the war-torn Europe of the nineteenth century, they were 410 lucky fellows. In fact, 410 must have been their lucky number, as we shall see.

But as the century drew to a close, the zinc reserves were fast running out, and with them the entire *raison d'être* of Neutral Moresnet. What would become of the place? The inhabitants realised that after squabbling over the place for so

---

[33] Otherwise known variously, though not always correctly, as hemimorphite or bonamite, or smithsonite after James Smithson (1764–1829), the British chemist whose money founded the Smithsonian Institution.

long, neither Belgium nor Prussia would want it, and some of them started campaigning to be incorporated into Belgium. One of the strongest suits (to borrow a metaphor from the gaming tables) of such microstates is often the ability to provide that which is banned in neighbouring countries, and for a while Altenberg was home to a profitable casino business. Gambling, once one of the great attractions of the Belgian town of Spa,[34] was by now banned in Belgium. But Neutral Moresnet was still governed by the Code Napoléon, under Article 410 of which gambling was not illegal if carried on in private, and so private gambling clubs became the order of the day – much to the displeasure of Belgium and Prussia, since neither wanted to see an international banking facility grow up on the slag heaps of this clapped-out mining community. With its parents unable to agree on anything, Child Moresnet played one off against the other and ran wild.

It even started to get ideas about being a proper country. In 1908 a novel proposal was put forward by one Wilhelm Molly, company doctor for the Altenberg mine, who had moved to Moresnet from his native Germany in 1863. He was a sort of Moresnetian patriot – if there can be such a thing in a place without a nationality – and had even issued stamps, though they were technically illegal and not recognised by either Belgium or Prussia. He was also a keen advocate of the artificial language, Esperanto, invented only twenty years before by Ludwig Zamenhof. What better destiny for his little corner of neutral territory at the heart of warring Europe, Molly suggested, than the world's first official Esperanto-speaking state? It would be called 'Amikejo', the friendship nation. A national anthem was composed and a flag devised, and the Esperantist Congress decided to move there from The Hague.

But it was war, not friendship, that was to provide the final resolution of this bizarre constitutional anomaly. The neutrality of Moresnet was blown away in the great cataclysm

[34] After which all spa towns are named.

of 1914, along with that of Belgium itself, when on 8 August German forces swept through on their way to Liège. At the end of the war most of Moresnet was awarded to Belgium under the terms of the Treaty of Versailles. Of course, that was not totally the end of the matter; more turmoil was to come in the next war, when Hitler annexed this and other German-speaking areas he considered had been stolen from the Fatherland. But Neutral Moresnet and its wild days, its mad existence, were a thing of the past.

North Britain

No, not just any northern bit of the UK. North Britain was at one time a commonly used name for Scotland.

What does it mean to be British? In historical and geographical terms of course, not philosophical or emotional ones. The word 'Britain' originally had a rather different sense to the one we know today. It referred to the Celtic inhabitants of these islands before the arrival of the Romans, who called it *Brittannia*[35]. Apparently the Celts themselves didn't really have a name for the whole British Isles, as opposed to the ethnic groups within it: Britain was not really a geographical concept.

Specifically, things British concerned the culture of the mainland Celts, as opposed to the Irish ones: the Brythonic (or Brittonic) tribes and languages, represented today by Welsh and Cornish, as opposed to the Goidelic (or Gaelic) ones of Ireland, Scotland and the Isle of Man. This British language was the ancestor of Welsh, at one time spoken all the way up through Cumbria and over much of lowland Scotland; thus, the Scottish Celts were originally Britons, but after invasions from Ireland became Gaels, at least in terms of language. Nevertheless, traces of British Celtic are still found in many place names, such as Dumbarton, spelled 'Dunbretane' in medieval times, the 'stronghold of the Britons'.

But then in the seventeenth and eighteenth centuries the word Britain came in very handy as a name for the newly unified nation of the English, Welsh and Scots (and later Irish). The Acts of Union of 1706 and 1707 decreed that 'the two Kingdoms of England and Scotland shall be united into one

---

[35] Note the two Ts and two Ns, a source of confusion ever since.

Kingdom by the Name of Great Britain', thus establishing the familiar (if confusing and often misused) term we know today.[36] Little Britain, when it's not the name of a popular TV comedy, is Brittany, more quaintly known as 'Britain the Less'. This Celtic bubble in northwest France is not a survival from antiquity, the home of Asterix the Gaul if you like, but the result of a much later colonial expedition from Cornwall.

The terms 'South-Brittains' and 'North-Brittains' for the English and the Scots had already been coined at the time of the Union of the Crowns in 1603, when the kingdoms of England and Scotland were united under James 'the Sixth of Scotland and the First of England' as 'King of Great Britain'. It seems fair to say that 'South Briton' never exactly caught on.[37] Nor did 'West Briton' for the Welsh, but the same term certainly had currency in the Irish context, and indeed still has. It's nearly always pejorative, meaning someone rather too sympathetic towards the colonial overlord. Conor Cruise O'Brien felt the term evoked 'a dentist's wife who collected crests, ate kedgeree for breakfast and displayed on her mantelpiece a portrait of the Dear Queen'. This excerpt from James Joyce's short story 'The Dead' gives the flavour:

– Well, I'm ashamed of you, said Miss Ivors frankly. To say you'd write for a rag like that. I didn't think you were a West Briton.

A look of perplexity appeared on Gabriel's face. It was true that he wrote a literary column every Wednesday in *The Daily Express*, for which he was paid fifteen shillings. But that did not make him a West Briton surely.

---

[36] So in a sense the words 'Britain' and 'British' have come to have almost the opposite of their original sense; whereas before they referred to the native Celts as opposed to the Roman or Germanic invaders, today they stress the union of all the (mostly non-Celtic) inhabitants of the UK, playing down the regional Celtic identity.

[37] 'South Britain' could have been the title of this article, but that would have been wilfully obscure.

But there were those who felt that the term West Briton had the merit of being more inclusive and that, to quote a letter written to Sir Robert Peel in 1816, the title of United Kingdom of Great Britain and Ireland served 'to remind people that they were once disunited and to keep them so – had the whole been called by one common name Britain . . . we West Britons would have been as much conciliated and attached as the North Britons are'.[38]

According to the *Oxford English Dictionary*, the term 'North Britain' is 'still in occasional (chiefly postal) use'. Well, perhaps so when those words were being drafted, nearly a century ago. The term seems to have been dimly remembered as late as the 1930s, to judge by an anecdote retailed by one H Teeling Smith, who sent a Christmas card from London to an address in Fife. Someone added the initials 'N. B.' to the envelope, and when the card eventually arrived – via Canada – it bore the words 'Try Scotland'. It had ended up in New Brunswick. In the time-honoured way, Mr Teeling Smith wrote a letter to *The Times* about it. 'Let this be a reminder to all,' he thundered, 'that the British postal authorities many years ago issued instructions that the letters N. B. must not be used as an abbreviation for North Britain.'

[38] With the benefit of hindsight, we might think that he spoiled it a bit with the last line, but although the Scots have not been so very 'conciliated and attached' in recent years, it's not quite the same as Ireland. We know what he means.

Batavia

There are fifty thousand hip baths in Batavia, and some of them are nearly five feet long. It's true – Kenneth Horne and Richard Murdoch sang about it in the surreal vintage radio comedy *Much-Binding-in-the-Marsh*. But where exactly are these hip baths? What is, or was, Batavia?

In ancient times, according to Tacitus, a Germanic tribe called the *Batavi* inhabited the Rhine Delta of Germany, more specifically the island of Betawe, between the Rhine and the Waal in what is now the Netherlands. Hence the Roman names of Leiden (*Lugdunum Batavorum*) and Nijmegen (*Batavodurum* or *Oppidum Batavorum*, later rebuilt as the grander *Ulpia Noviomagus Batavorum*). Thus *Batavia* has long served as the Latin name of the Netherlands, or a poetic synonym: 'flat Batavia's willowy groves' Wordsworth called them.

Batavis, *Castra Batavorum* and *Castra Batava* are Latin names for Passau – a city in Eastern Bavaria, which is a long way from the historical Batavia – because Batavian troops were once stationed there. The Romans had a policy of not allowing native troops to serve within their province of origin, after a rebellion in Batavia in AD 69–70 led by Gaius Julius Civilis, who managed to capture two dozen ships and destroy four whole legions. Batavian cohorts were also among those that manned the forts along Hadrian's Wall.

When the Netherlands acquired their Southeast Asian empire during the seventeenth century, they made their base at a port called Sunda Kelapa or Jayakarta, and christened it Batavia. Of course we know it now as Jakarta, capital and largest city of the modern state of Indonesia. There's still a Batavia in the former Dutch colonial territory in South

America, Suriname,[39] but it's not a big place. Naturally the USA has a few Batavias[40] as well, in such places as Indiana, Illinois, Ohio and New York State.

Batavia was the name of a ship of the Dutch East India Company, built in Amsterdam in 1628. On her maiden voyage, bound for the East Indies, she was wrecked off the inhospitable coast of Western Australia. Her commander decided to continue to Batavia to fetch help, an epic journey of nearly five weeks in a 30-foot longboat, but in his absence some of the senior officers mutinied. They instituted a reign of terror among the surviving passengers and crew, killing, torturing and raping dozens before finally being arrested by the returning rescue party. Of the hundreds who set off on board the *Batavia*, scarcely one in five arrived in the city of that name.

The name was pressed into service once again in 1795, in the wake of the French Revolution, when something called the Batavian Republic was proclaimed in the Netherlands. The old provinces were replaced by new 'departments' in the French manner, with a National Assembly to which deputies were elected directly, and freedom of religion for all including Roman Catholics and Jews. But the Netherlands was still under French occupation, and in reality this 'protectorate' was more of a puppet state than a true national Republic. Not only did all decisions have to be approved by Paris, but heavy financial tribute was extracted in the form of what we might now call stealth taxes. After barely a decade it was reformed as the Batavian Commonwealth under a kind of viceroy with absolute power; the following year it became the Kingdom of Holland once more, under Napoleon's brother Louis; and in 1810 the Netherlands were incorporated fully into the French Empire.

What else is Batavia famous for? Batavian fever, a form of leptospirosis . . . Batavia, a kind of shot silk, apparently made in a twill weave on four harnesses . . . and all those hip baths, of course. They wouldn't say it on the wireless if it wasn't true, would they?

[39] Dutch Guiana as was.
[40] Bataviæ?

British Heligoland

International geopolitics makes for strange bedfellows. The 1890 Heligoland–Zanzibar Treaty (or Anglo-German Agreement), for example – what linked an East African island with one in the chilly North Sea?

The wonderfully named Heligoland[41] is an outcrop of sandstone and chalk[42] in the North Sea, about fifty miles off the German coast, only half a square mile in area but strategically placed with respect to the Kiel Canal and the Rivers Elbe and Weser. If you are of a certain age, you may remember it from the shipping forecast on what you used to call the wireless.[43]

It's another of those odd little places with a complex identity and a disproportionately lively history. 'Heligo-landers!' declared Sir Henry Berkeley Fitzhardinge Maxse, Governor from 1864 to 1881, 'your island is circumscribed, your population is small, but you are still a nation in yourself.' Heligoland may be German today but its history is largely Danish, as part of the much-disputed province of Schleswig-Holstein, and its inhabitants are historically Friesians[44] speaking a Heligolandic dialect called Halunder. The British seized the island from the Danes in 1807 to use as a base against Napoleon, and it was formally ceded to Britain in 1814 under the Treaty of Kiel.

But valuable as this base was, it ended up a bargaining chip in the scramble for Africa, traded for Zanzibar (then under

---

[41] Helgoland in German, supposedly from *Heyligeland*, 'Holy Land'.
[42] The same chalk that forms the famous white cliffs of Dover. A combination of quarrying and violent storms had destroyed most of it by the 18th century.
[43] It's now known by the more general term of German Bight.
[44] People, of course, not black-and-white cows.

German control) along with what became Tanganyika, which contains within its borders Mount Kilimanjaro – and thereby hangs a charming tale. The border dividing what is now Kenya from Tanzania is ruler-straight, except for a little kink skirting north around Kilimanjaro. This, so the story goes, is because the Kaiser complained that Britain had two African mountains and Germany none. So Queen Victoria simply made a present of Africa's highest peak to the Kaiser – who was, of course, her grandson.[45]

British rule might have come to an end, but the British had not by any means finished with Heligoland. In August 1914 the Battle of Heligoland Bight was the first naval engagement of the Great War and a decisive victory for Britain. 'We're on our way to Heligoland,' went the song, 'To get the Kaiser's goat, In a good old Yankee boat, Up the Kiel canal we'll float. I'm a son of a gun, if I see a Hun I'll make him understand, I'll knock the Heligo, Into Heligo, Out of Heligoland!' At the end of the war all the harbours and defensive positions were ordered put beyond use in perpetuity under Article 115 of the Versailles Treaty – and that was not the last battering the island was to receive.

On 18 April 1945 poor Heligoland was the target of a gigantic air raid, when over a thousand Allied bombers pulverised the place into dust and ashes. But even worse was to come: the now uninhabited island was again occupied by

---

[45] Is it true? No, of course not.

British forces and used as a bombing range. There followed a deliberate attempt to destroy the island completely in 1947, using several thousand tons of war-surplus explosive to produce one of the largest non-nuclear explosions in history. Heligoland is still there, most of it, but the 'Big Bang' altered its shape for good.

When Germany finally regained possession in 1952 a huge task of munitions clearance, landscaping and rebuilding lay ahead before it could be repopulated. But today resilient little Heligoland is once again a thriving community, visited by thousands of tourists a day in the summer. They go there for the clean air and spectacular scenery, not to mention the duty-free,[46] and to travel the 200 feet or so between the upper and lower towns in a special lift manned by a uniformed attendant. It really is amazing what punishment a good strong piece of sandstone can take.

---

[46] Though no longer to gamble as they once did, before that was made illegal in 1870.

Londonderry

That very name may set a few teeth grinding. It's hard even to refer to that historic city on the banks of the Foyle without seeming to take sides in a rivalry, perhaps we might even say a war, that has been grumbling away for three centuries. Britain's Macedonia, perhaps. To simplify, at the risk of more grinding teeth, the Unionists traditionally call it Londonderry, and the Republicans call it Derry. Where that leaves the rest of us is a matter of debate and potential embarrassment.

The ancient settlement of Derry, in Irish *Doire*, is first heard of in the sixth century when St Columba founded a monastery there. Fuller names attribute this oak-grove to Columba (*Doire Cholm Cille*) or before him an ancient warlord called Calgach (*Daire Calgaich*). The name Derry comes from a Celtic word for the oak tree, which is also the origin of the word 'druid', as well as place names such as Kildare and Derwent. During the 'plantation'[47] of Ulster with English and Scottish settlers during the seventeenth century, rights and privileges were granted by the British Crown over various Irish assets. One such was when in 1613 James I granted a charter to the representatives of the City of London livery companies for the construction of a walled city at Derry. The name Londonderry was coined for the redesigned city – and that, you might say, is where the trouble (and the Troubles) started.

The gates of the city were closed against the Jacobite army during the siege of 1688, which lasted 105 days until King Billy's cavalry came over the metaphorical hill. This is the origin of the nickname 'the Maiden City', and explains (to some extent) why portly middle-aged men in Orange sashes, who are

---

[47] No tree pun intended.

neither boys nor apprentices, call themselves Apprentice Boys for the purposes of marching and banging drums. The famous mural welcomes them to the Catholic Bogside with the words 'You Are Now Entering Free Derry'.

So what policy should, for example, the BBC adopt in these supposedly enlightened and culturally sensitive times? You can't go through the whole sorry tale every time you want to refer to the place. People tread carefully round the issue; the local radio station is BBC Radio Foyle, and signs sometimes use the formula DERRY/LONDONDERRY, pronounced 'Derry Stroke Londonderry', which gives rise to the jocular nickname 'Stroke City'. The Northern Irish broadcaster Gerry Anderson is probably responsible for introducing this soubriquet into the mainland British consciousness when he used it as the title of his quirky radio talks about everyday life in the Province.

Linguistic confusion doesn't rank with bombings and shootings, but it makes life very difficult nonetheless. Puzzled tourists ask you how long it takes to get from Derry to Londonderry. Better-informed visitors worry that using the wrong name in the wrong company may get them beaten up. Not even having a title that everyone can agree on is hardly good news when it comes to trying to attract inward investment for a new era of peace and prosperity. Brand identity, people!

It's sometimes said[48] that nowadays Londonderry is used by only a minority of Unionists, often in a provocative spirit, but the term is far from dead. Catholics may be in a three-to-one majority there, but the 'official' name is still Londonderry, and that is what most people on the mainland know it as. The main association the word has for them is probably the 'Troubles', specifically the infamous 'Bloody Sunday' shootings of 1972. It can hardly sound anything but sinister. Is it time to do away with 'Londonderry' once and for all?

That is certainly the view of a determined campaign to

---

[48] Though not by this author, who must remain strictly neutral on that point, out of both ignorance and pusillanimity.

change the city's name officially to Derry, apparently the first time such a thing has been attempted in the UK. A judicial review, no less, started at the end of 2006 to look into the question – not an easy matter legally, since royal charters cannot lightly be done away with. The supporters of the name-change claim that the charter 'created a municipal corporation but didn't give a name to a physical location'. Perhaps, by the time you read this, the name 'Londonderry' will be officially redundant, and will actually deserve its place in this book.[49] Or perhaps we'll still have to pick our way between Derry, Doire, Doire Cholm Cille, Daire Calgaich Calgach, the Walled City, the Maiden City, Stroke City – and Londonderry.

[49] It's a calculated gamble.

Rangoon

'In Rangoon, the heat of noon is just what the natives shun,' sang Noël Coward. 'They put their Scotch or rye down, and lie down.' A name as mellifluous as Rangoon must be a gift to any songwriter. It reminds us of such exotic-sounding words as doubloon, dragoon, baboon and typhoon. One can just picture an immaculately dressed Hercule Poirot reclining on a rattan chair in some elegant watering hole, whiling away the rainy season with card games: a Walloon playing pontoon in the saloon during the monsoon.

In fact 'Rangoon' is a distortion of the Burmese Yangon, to which it officially reverted in 1989 – a name which had itself been imposed during the eighteenth century on a village then known as Dagon. There is perhaps a trace of irony in the fact that *yangon* means something like 'no more enemies'. Since the name was changed by a military dictatorship with very little official recognition among the international community, the change from Rangoon to Yangon, just like that of Burma to Myanmar, has been far from universally adopted, and whatever the country lacks at present it is not enemies.

But despite a couple of tsunamis and a world war, Rangoon remains one of the most beautiful cities in Asia. Palaces and pagodas mingle with a wealth of fine colonial architecture still capable of evoking the era when mad dogs and Englishmen would, if the song is to be believed, go out in the midday sun. Mandalay, incidentally, is still Mandalay, though whether the dawn really does come up like thunder our sources do not record.

Leopoldville

In 1933, the French illustrator Jean de Brunhoff published *Le Roi Babar*, the third of his stories about a genial talking elephant. After a time in Paris under the tutelage of a benevolent old lady, Babar returns to Africa with his elephant wife Celeste and a consignment of Western consumer durables, and sets about building a city. He rallies his tribe with these words: 'My friends, in these trunks[50] and bales and cases I have presents for all of you – dresses, hats, silks, paint-boxes, drums, tins of peaches, feathers, racquets, and many other things. I will give them to you as soon as we have built our new town. This town, the town of the elephants, I propose that we call Celesteville in honour of your Queen.' The elephants go on to construct a model Western capital, with full employment and impressive cultural and leisure facilities. 'The Palace of Work is next to the Palace of Pleasure, which is very convenient.'[51]

The advent in Africa of King Leopold II of the Belgians[52] was not so warm-hearted. The *Roi-Bâtisseur* or Builder-King was determined that Belgium should have a colony. West Africa had been thoroughly explored and colonised since the fifteenth century; the race was on for the basin of the mighty Congo, the 'river to swallow up all rivers', and the French were moving in. Their man on the ground was one Pierre-Paul-François-Camille Savorgnan de Brazza, a naturalised

---

[50] Remember that this story was originally written in French and there was no pun intended.

[51] Theorists, as theorists will, have looked at King Babar's suits and spats, his autocratic regime and his westernising policies, and seen a repellent apologia for neo-colonialism. Others say it's just a children's story.

[52] Or rather, of his envoys, since he never went there himself.

Frenchman born in Italy. In 1881 he planted his flag at the spot known to this day as Brazzaville and staked the claim to Middle Congo (now the Republic of Congo), which would later became part of French Equatorial Africa, along with Gabon, Chad and Oubangui-Chari (now the Central African Republic).

Since the Belgian state seemed to have no great interest in joining the so-called Scramble for Africa, King Leopold had decided to do the job himself. In 1876 he founded the

Association Internationale Africaine, a strictly humanitarian organisation with the highest ideals, to 'carry to the interior of Africa new ideas of law, order, humanity and protection of the natives', in the words of the *Daily Telegraph* in 1884; or, as Leopold himself put it privately, to carve out a slice of the *'magnifique gâteau africain'*.[53] He recruited Henry Morton Stanley, among others, to begin the advancement of the poor benighted Congolese by schmoozing local potentates and quietly staking out territory.

Then came the Berlin (or Congo) Conference of 1884–5, a sort of regulatory framework whereby the European super-powers[54] carved up the African cake between themselves, and which recognised Leopold's claim to what became known as

[53] A fine philanthropic phrase.
[54] No African representative was present even as an observer.

the Congo Free State, *l'État Indépendant du Congo*. Its capital was Leopoldville (*Léopoldville* in French, *Leopoldstad* in Dutch). Suddenly, and all by accident of course, Leopold found himself the de facto owner – not the administrator or trustee or company director or colonial overlord or even king, but the owner in his own personal capacity – of getting on for a million square miles of central Africa,[55] surely the largest private estate ever 'owned' by any individual. It's difficult to comprehend the potential wealth that represented, in terms of natural resources like ivory and, with the coming of electricity and pneumatic tyres, copper and rubber. The officers of the Association Internationale redoubled their civilising efforts and philanthropised with ruthless efficiency and hippopotamus-hide whips. They imposed a system of forced labour, really a form of slavery, whereby crippling production quotas were enforced with incredible brutality and contempt for human life. In order to discourage wastage of ammunition, overseers had to produce, for every shot fired, the severed hand of the recipient of that round. Thus the human hand actually functioned as a form of currency, since it could pay for bullets and make up shortfalls in ivory or rubber quotas.

Stories of these atrocities started to circulate in Europe, not least through Joseph Conrad's novella *Heart of Darkness* (1902), whose narrator signs up with an international trading company in Brussels as a steamboat captain, and soon finds himself travelling upriver calling at 'places with farcical names, where the merry dance of death and trade goes on', and where 'bundles of acute angles sat with their legs drawn up'. No one will ever know how many millions of lives were lost in the merry dance, but estimates vary all the way from three to thirty million.[56] These lines by the American poet Vachel Lindsay, a forerunner of the jazz poets, seem to capture the diabolical jollity of that dance:

[55] About 75 times the size of Belgium.
[56] The modern population of Belgium is about ten million.

> Listen to the yell of Leopold's ghost
> Burning in Hell for his hand-maimed host
> Hear how the demons chuckle and yell
> Cutting his hands off, down in Hell.

Roger Casement, then British Consul in the Congo, submitted a damning report on the horror, and in 1908 after much deliberation the Belgian government confiscated – or rather bought for a couple of million pounds – the Congo Free State from the King of the Belgians. It became the Belgian Congo, and remained so until independence in 1960 as Congo-Leopoldville. The hippopotamus-hide whips were made illegal in 1955.

The map of Central Africa was still generously larded with villes, some of which names, such as Brazzaville in the Republic of Congo and Franceville in Gabon, have survived. Those in the ex-Belgian Congo, however, were done away with in 1966 by President Mobutu Sese Seko as part of the process of 'Zairianisation'. Leopoldville changed to Kinshasa, Elisabethville to Lubumbashi, Stanleyville to Kisangani, and the rather lesser-known Jadotville[57] to Likasi. Celesteville is, as far as history records, entirely fictional.

---

[57] After the Belgian mining engineer Jean Jadot (1862–1932).

Transcaspia

In the stark landscape of the Cold War, the Soviet Union tended to be seen as a monolithic bloc of Slavdom looming over the 'Free World'. In fact it was often inaccurately referred to as 'Russia', much as people use the word 'England' to mean the United Kingdom, even though Russia occupied only three quarters of the area of this huge and complex confederation, 'a riddle wrapped in a mystery inside an enigma', as Churchill described it.[58] Some of the peripheral republics, such as the Baltic states, were only briefly part of the Soviet bloc; others were recent creations in places where the nation state such as we picture it in the West had never existed. Old atlases show them for what they were: vast expanses of largely empty, semi-charted desert, whose nomadic peoples fell nominally under the sway of Persians or Turks or Mongols or Russians or whoever was strong at the time.

One such place was Transcaspia, east of the Caspian and south of the Aral Sea, on the western fringe of that great sprawling expanse known as Turkestan, the area of Central Asia inhabited by Turkic-speaking peoples such as the Uzbeks and Azeris and Tatars. It was conquered by the Russians in 1881 and became the Transcaspian Province; then in 1918 the province of Transcaspia, then in 1924 the Turkmen Soviet Socialist Republic. Since 1991 we have known it as the Republic of Turkmenistan or Turkmenia.

Africa and India offer strong competition, but it is surely the Soviet Bloc countries that take the biscuit for number and frequency of name-changes – and not just bureaucratic technicalities the general populace could happily ignore, as the

---

[58] Even though he called it Russia too.

British public rightly does with ridiculous rebrandings like 'Consignia' for the Post Office[59] or the privatised railway company, formerly London Eastern Railway Ltd, that has taken to calling itself 'one'.[60] Using the wrong name was sometimes actually illegal and could get you into trouble.

Saparmurat Atayevich Niyazov, President of Turkmenistan since 1990, died suddenly just before Christmas 2006. You may have been too busy shopping to notice but in Turkmenistan it must have seemed like the end of the world as they knew it. Since Soviet times this man had been the leader and figurehead of the nation, an old-style tin-pot dictator if ever there was one. Admittedly, he successfully stood for re-election in 1992, but then again he was the only candidate.

The Niyazov personality cult is symbolised by something called the holy Ruhnama or 'Book of the Soul'. It's a sort of equivalent of Mao's 'little red book', described[61] as 'a mix of folklore, morality, autobiography and history written in oracular style'. Not only does it form a major part of the school curriculum, but getting a driving licence involves sixteen hours of Ruhnama study, 'to ensure future drivers are educated in the spirit of high moral values of Turkmenistan's society'. Doubtless it was for the same reasons that the 'light of new Turkmen literature' banned video games, opera, ballet, car radios, smoking in the street, long hair and beards (for young men), make-up (for newsreaders) and gold teeth.[62]

In true Big Brother style, his image is everywhere – 'I don't take any pleasure in it,' he claimed, 'but the people demand it' – and never more visibly so than atop the 250-foot 'Neutrality Arch', the tallest building in the Turkmen capital, Aşgabat, complete with panoramic glass lift. At the top is a rotating bronze statue of the President, covered with 23-carat gold leaf; it rotates

[59] From 2000 to 2002.
[60] In 2006 (and this is truly irrelevant) it gained the dubious distinction of running the nation's most overcrowded train service, the infamous 08:02 from Cambridge to Liverpool Street.
[61] By Reuters, the news agency.
[62] Instead he recommended chewing on bones as the best way to dental health.

once every 24 hours in order to be seen from all directions.

He also had a dictator's way with names, styling himself 'Türkmenbaşy' ('Leader of the Turkmen People'), and renaming things after himself in the time-honoured manner. One of several places he baptised Türkmenbaşy was Krasnovodsk on the Caspian coast, where the Russians had built a fort in 1869 as a base for their campaigns against Khiva and Bukhara. The old name is a Russification of the original name Kyzyl-Su, which means 'Red Water', presumably that of the Krasnovodsk Gulf which bathes the city. It's an important place to this day, being the site of Turkmenistan's largest oil refinery, the western terminus of the Trans-Caspian Railway, and Central Asia's only sea link to Europe.

It wasn't just places: even the days of the week and months of the year were renamed, after Turkmen national symbols specified in the Ruhnama. January (*ýanwar*) became *Türkmenbaşy*, September (*Sentýabr*) became *Ruhnama*, and April (*Aprel*) was renamed *Gurbansoltan* after a woman called Gurbansoltan Eje. And who was she? She was the President-for-Life's own dear mother. Nice gesture. If only all sons were in a position to be so generous.

Spanish Sahara

One of the sorest bones of diplomatic contention between Spain and Britain has been Gibraltar. For many years the British presence was felt as an intolerable insult to Spanish national pride and even today, in the post-Franco era when we're all supposed to be the best of friends, it is a sensitive subject, with allegations that Gibraltar presents a soft target to cigarette- and people-smugglers.

The Spanish seem to see no irony in the fact that their colonial presence in North Africa is not only so recent, but indeed far from over. They retain two enclaves on the Moroccan coast, Ceuta and Melilla, disputed by Morocco, and recently actually sent troops to defend the tiny Mediterranean island of Perejil[63] against an experimental Moroccan incursion.

But of course this is nothing compared to the extent of Spanish influence in Africa in the late nineteenth century and most of the twentieth. Until 1969, some thirteen years after Morocco gained independence, Spain retained control over the enclave of Sidi Ifni on the southwest Atlantic Coast. Spanish presence in the area goes back ultimately to 1476 and a settlement called Santa Cruz de la Mar Pequeña ('The Holy Cross of the Little Sea'), from where slaves were shipped to the Canaries; its exact location is uncertain but was reinvented as Sidi Ifni when Spain wished to assert its claim to the southern Sahara.

Under the terms of the Berlin Conference of 1884–5, which

---

[63] Population: a few goats. Its name refers to the wild parsley they feed on. Other such tiny island territories off the Moroccan coast still 'owned' by Spain are Alborán, the Peñón de Vélez de la Gomera, the Peñón de Alhucemas ('Lavender Rock') and the three Islas Chafarinas.

regulated the so-called Scramble for Africa by the European powers, Spain gained control over vast expanses of the northwestern coast of Africa, and joined it up with its existing possessions of Saguía el-Hamra[64] in the north and Río de Oro[65] in the south, to make Spanish Sahara. This was a separate territory from the protectorate of Spanish Morocco, about 500 miles to the north, which stretched along the Mediterranean coast from around Tangier (under international administration from 1923 to 1956) through Ceuta (opposite Gibraltar) to Melilla in the east.

In the declining years of the Franco regime, Spain came under increasing international pressure to decolonise, as well as suffering guerrilla attacks from the newly formed (1973) 'Polisario Front' or Frente Popular de *Liberación de Saguía el Hamra y Río de Oro*.[66] Morocco was very close to the heart of Spanish Nationalists, none more so than the 'Generalissimo' himself, since it was there that he had cut his teeth as a military commander, coming within an ace of dying from a bullet wound in the process. The fanatical loyalty he inspired in both Spanish and Moroccan troops, forged by means of iron discipline and a determination always to suffer the same dangers and privations as his men, was crucial both

[64] Literally 'Red Canal'.
[65] 'Gold River'.
[66] 'Popular Front for the Liberation of Saguía el-Hamra and Río de Oro'.

to Franco's rapid rise to prominence and his subsequent victory in the Civil War.[67]

But by the 1970s things were changing fast in Spain, a country in the process of shaking off the dead hand of dictatorship, and it finally relinquished 'Spanish' Sahara in 1976. Both Morocco and Mauritania promptly moved in to claim it, despite a ruling by the International Court of Justice that the Sahrawi (Saharawi) people had the right of self-determination, and the Sahrawi Arab Democratic Republic declared by the Polisario stood no chance against such superior forces. Mauritania, itself no superpower, withdrew its claim in 1979, and it is Morocco that controls most of Western Sahara today, with much of the Sahrawi nation living in exile in refugee camps in Algeria.

During the 1980s Moroccan forces moved steadily south from the capital Laâyoune (*El Aaiún* to the Spanish), securing their gains as they went by means of something called the Moroccan Wall or Berm: huge sand and stone fortifications stretching over 1,500 miles, complete with landmines, radar tank-tops and everything the modern world can do to separate one piece of desert from another. Why is Morocco so keen to secure this barren sandscape? As well as rich fishing grounds, the berm protects the phosphate mines of Boucraa (Boukra), where the product is shipped out all the way to the coast on a conveyor belt said to be the longest in the world.

By the mid-1980s over sixty countries had recognised Polisario as the legitimate government, and a ceasefire was declared in 1991 on the understanding that a referendum would be carried out on the future of the country. This process has stalled on the issue of who should be allowed to vote – the

---

[67] He was also one of the founding members of the Tercio de Extranjeros or Spanish Foreign Legion, a body of men which supposedly made the French model look like a Sunday-school outing. These *novios de la muerte* or 'bridegrooms of death' were part of the cult of toughness and brutality that lay at the heart of the Franco myth. Their action in opening fire on a pro-Sahrawi independence demonstration in 1970 triggered an intifada and hastened the end of Spanish rule.

current population of the territory, which includes many Moroccan settlers and excludes all the Polisario supporters exiled in Algeria, or those who were resident when the Moroccans invaded. Polisario has repeatedly threatened to resume hostilities, but for the moment the ceasefire holds; and meanwhile the influence of the widely recognised legitimate government-in-exile of Western Sahara is restricted to the inland desert areas. Not for the first time in history, one colonial power has simply been replaced by another.

Henpeck

Here's a story you've probably heard before. There's a place in the state of Illinois, in Crawford County to be precise, that goes by the unusual name of Oblong.[68] As a matter of fact it claims to be the only place of that name in the world.[69] A man from the rather larger town of Normal, Illinois[70] goes there for some reason and meets the girl of his dreams. Soon they are going steady and decide to get hitched. The headline in the local paper runs: 'Normal man weds Oblong woman'.

In America there are 'incorporated' places and unincorporated ones. The latter sort, also known as census-designated places or CDPs, have no municipal government and are administered as a part of some larger division such as a state. By the time a new settlement achieves a certain size or importance, it often chooses to 'incorporate', i.e. form a corporation and govern itself. Often this change in status seems to come along with a name change. For example, Normal is right next to the rather better-known Bloomington, Illinois, and used to be known boringly enough as North Bloomington. It was home to Illinois State Normal University, a teacher-training college, and when it incorporated, in 1865, it chose to show off its academic credentials by adopting the stylish name 'Normal'.

But this is pretty small beer when it comes to small towns in North America with bizarre names. Humptulips,

[68] Population: 1,491.
[69] However, there is a strange little strip of Connecticut called The Oblong, also known as Connecticut's panhandle or more sinisterly 'the handle of the cleaver'.
[70] Population: 4,206.

Washington[71] and Unalaska, Alaska[72] are two of this author's favourites, and rumours of a place in Wyoming called Maggie's Nipples seem credible.[73] People will also rename their towns after all sort of nonsense. Caney Creek, Kentucky[74] was renamed 'Pippa Passes' after Robert Browning's poem of that name,[75] and in 1993 Ismay, Montana[76] wittily restyled itself 'Joe, Montana' after the famous NFL quarterback. Often these things are no more than publicity stunts: Hot Springs, New Mexico took the name 'Truth or Consequences' in 1950, after a popular radio programme of that name, in response to a kind of dare from the host of the show; in December 1999, at the height of the so-called dot.com boom, a place called Halfway, Oregon accepted an offer to rename itself 'Half.com' in exchange for $100,000 worth of computer equipment. Clark, Texas, all 55 households of it, rebranded itself 'DISH'[77] in return for free satellite television for ten years.[78]

A strong competitor for the weirdest name in America must surely be a settlement out in the Mojave Desert of California called Zzyzx[79]. It's pronounced 'ZYE-ziks'.[80] It was a spa and health resort founded in 1944 by one Curtis Howe Springer, an American radio evangelist who claimed to be a doctor and Methodist minister but was neither. He wanted it to be, you've guessed it, the last word in both luxury and the English language. He staked his claim to the land and, before it had even been accepted, had built his health spa; as well as mineral baths and a sixty-room hotel it had a church, a private airstrip

---

[71] Population: 49,508.

[72] Population: 248.

[73] In fairness Britain must own up to Wallish Walls, Twice Brewed, Pity Me and Wetwang as well as the famous Nempnett Thrubwell.

[74] Population: 293.

[75] 'God's in His heaven, all's right with the world', etc.

[76] Population: 25.

[77] The capital letters were part of the deal.

[78] Apparently twelve citizens attended the meeting to support the measure; the rest presumably had something on the telly they couldn't miss.

[79] Not to be confused with *Zyzzyx*, which as you know is a genus of sand wasp.

[80] Obviously.

and a radio station over which to advertise health drinks – and apparently a castle of some kind. Things fell apart somewhat when he was convicted of false advertising and squatting on federal land. It's now the Desert Studies Center, used among others by scientists studying an endangered fish species called the Mohave tui chub (*Gila bicolor mohavensis*).

So here's another story. Who knows, maybe it's true. There was once a little one-horse town in Illinois, nothing much more than a crossroads with a general store run by a man called Henry Peck. The sign above the shop said 'HEN. PECK', and thus the spot came to be known locally as Henpeck. When the town acquired its second horse the time had clearly come to step up to the plate and incorporate. 'Henpeck' wouldn't do as the name, so they cast around for a better one. They drew up the plans, took one look at the shape of their new municipality, and – eureka! – Oblong was born. It's the only one in the world, you know.

Ceylon

We know it as Sri Lanka now, of course, the ancient Sanskrit name found in the Mahabharata that has been used since 1972, but this 'resplendent island' has had many names. The full Sinhalese name is Sri Lanka Prajathanthrika Samajavadi Janarajaya. A slightly different form, Siri Laka, was said to be the preference of the former Sri Lankan president Ranasinghe Premadasa. The Tamils use the name Ilankai. Ceylon is the anglicised version of the Portuguese name of Ceilão (ultimately from the same *sinha*, or lion, that gives us the name of the island's dominant ethnic group, the Sinhalese). Yet other names include Heladiva, Heladveepa, Lankadweepa, Lakbima . . . add in a myriad different spellings of the same names and you begin to wonder whether 'Island of a Thousand Names' might be appropriate. The Ancient Greeks knew it as Salike or Simundu, or Taprobane (from the Pali word Tambaparni, of dubious origin). The Chinese supposedly named it Pa-Outchow or 'Isle of Gems'. The Arabs called it Tenerisim ('Delightful Island'), or Singal-Dip or Sarandib, another lion-based name from which we have the Persian Serendip. If that one rings a kind of faint bell, it may be because the word has entered the English language, to mean something quite unrelated to islands or lions.

The word in question is serendipity: the experience of stumbling upon something that was not what you were looking for, but perhaps was more worth having than the thing you wanted. The origins of most words are, if not quite lost in the mists of time, at least shrouded in them, but in this case we know exactly who invented it, as well as where the idea came from and what the name of a South Asian island has to do with it. It was coined by Horace Walpole, who wrote on 28 January

1754 that 'this discovery, indeed, is almost of that kind which I call Serendipity, a very expressive word'. He named it after an old Persian fairy tale about the 'Three Princes of Serendip', who, as he explained in a letter of 1754, 'were always making discoveries, by accidents and sagacity, of things they were not in quest of'. It's a useful concept, especially in experimental science, where it can be important not to disregard an unexpected result or discovery because it is not directly relevant. A classic example would be Alexander Fleming's batch of specimens 'ruined' by mould – a mould that gave us penicillin and changed the world.[81]

The 'discovery' of America by explorers looking for the Indies has been described as 'the greatest serendipity of history'. From the point of view of the discoverers at least.

---

[81] Presumably that makes him a 'serendipitist' – James Joyce's coinage. Trust him to go one better.

Zaire

The Belgians withdrew from 'their' Congo in 1960, signing off with a farewell speech from King Baudouin praising Leopold II and sorrowfully detailing Belgium's noble philanthropic donations to the country.[82] The prime minister of this First Republic of the Congo, or Congo-Léopoldville, was Patrice Lumumba, a passionate nationalist who failed to tame this enormous and volatile 'state without a nation' containing many dozens of different tribal groups. Faced with a Belgian-backed rebellion in the southern province of Katanga, he sought Soviet aid and hence put himself on the wrong side of the Americans – becoming, allegedly, the target of an assassination attempt by the CIA using poisoned toothpaste.[83] Certainly the US was on record as wanting rid of him. But before the hitman could get there Lumumba was toppled in a military coup. He was imprisoned, beaten up and humiliated on film. When he tried to escape, he was put up against tree and shot by a firing squad directed, so it seems, by Belgian army officers. His body was buried on the spot, but later dug up[84] and dissolved in acid, the bones being ground up and scattered to the winds to make absolutely sure there was nothing left of him.

Behind this coup was Lumumba's own state president, Joseph Kasavubu, backed by – and in turn soon deposed by – a certain Colonel Joseph-Désiré Mobutu, later known as

[82] Of course, these had been paid for with a very small portion of the riches looted from that same country.

[83] Truth is so often stranger than fiction, and poisoned toothpaste is no more bizarre than the range of clandestine devices said to have been deployed by the CIA against Fidel Castro, from exploding cigars to a poison designed to make his beard fall out.

[84] By a Belgian police commissioner.

Mobutu Sese Seko. Or, to give it the full honorifics, Mobutu Sese Seko Nkuku Ngbendu wa Za Banga: 'the all-powerful warrior who through persistence and resolve goes from conquest to conquest leaving fire in his wake'. In the interests of African 'authenticity' he actually outlawed European Christian names under pain of imprisonment. He also banned Western influences such as skin-bleaching, hair-straightening, foreign music and so on, and even invented a new form of suitably authentic formal attire: the 'abacost', short for '*à bas le costume*' or 'down with the business suit'. It's a kind of lightweight Mao-style number[85] worn open-necked or with a cravat (neckties being banned), and in the case of the dictator himself, teamed with the trademark leopard-skin hat.

This 'Zairianisation' also served to justify the imposition of dictatorship. As Mobutu put it, '*dans notre tradition africaine, il n'y a jamais deux chefs*'.[86] In 1991 he declared: 'The chief is the chief. He is the eagle who flies high and cannot be touched by the spit of the toad.'[87]

---

[85] 'Safari suit' would sound too colonial.

[86] 'In our African tradition, there are never two chiefs.'

[87] Presumably he had in mind the French proverb '*La bave du crapaud n'atteint pas la blanche colombe*', roughly equivalent to 'Sticks and stones may break my bones . . .', though perhaps Shakespeare's 'Nice customs curtsey to great kings' gets closer in this case.

The familiar symptoms emerged: an absurd personality cult, rampant corruption and nepotism, hyperinflation caused by literally printing money, and the institutionalised theft of vast sums of public money to spend on personal extravagances while the country rotted and life expectancy sank below pre-independence levels. According to Paul Vallely, the veteran reporter and governmental adviser on Africa, 'Mobutu's extravagance was legendary. He had villas, ranches, palaces and yachts throughout Europe. Concorde was constantly hired. He didn't just have Swiss bank accounts; he bought a Swiss bank. He didn't just get his wife a Mercedes; he bought a Mercedes assembly plant for her.' Supposedly the billions he stashed away during this 'kleptocracy' could almost have paid off the vast national debt.

But the stability he imposed made him flavour of the decade with the Americans, and his country was a useful conduit for the channelling of supplies to Jonas Savimbi in his campaign against the Marxist government of Angola.[88] During one of Mobutu's visits to the White House, Ronald Reagan described him as 'a voice of good sense and goodwill'.[89]

Mobutu it was who in 1971 changed the name of the country to Zaire, which is said to come from a fifteenth-century Portuguese mangling of a local Kikongo word for the river. In 1997, after Mobutu's defeat by Laurent-Désiré Kabila, the name was changed back to Congo. Since there already was a Republic (previously People's Republic) of Congo, the ex-French one whose capital is still called Brazzaville after the Franco-Italian explorer Savorgnan de Brazza, it is officially known as the Democratic Republic of Congo (DRC). A more user-friendly and less bureaucratic-sounding way of referring to them is Congo-Kinshasa and Congo-Brazzaville.

But Mobutu's sad legacy of neglect and decay was responsible for another name-change, albeit unofficial.

---

[88] Supplies worth $25 million, according to a former head of the CIA in Zaire.
[89] For all its pious worship of democracy, American foreign policy loves nothing better than a 'useful tyrant'.

Kinshasa, considered one of Africa's cleanest and most elegant cities, was nicknamed '*Kin la Belle*'. With piles of refuse clogging the streets, it became *Kin la Poubelle* – 'Kinshasa the Dustbin'.

Pepys Island

It's not so much that Pepys Island no longer exists; in fact, it never existed. It's a phantom island. Or is it? Bear with me.

In 1683 Captain William Ambrose Cowley, travelling with William Dampier, described finding an island off the coast of Chile that he named after the then Secretary of the Admiralty, Samuel Pepys:

> We held our Course S. W. till we came into the lat. of 47 deg. where we saw Land; the same being an Island not before known, lying to the Westward of us. It was not inhabited, and I gave it the Name of Pepys Island. We found it a very commodious place for Ships to water at and take in Wood, and it has a very good Harbour, where a thousand sail of Ships may safely ride: Here is great plenty of Fowls, and we judge, abundance of Fish, by reason of the Grounds [sea-floor] being nothing but Rocks and Sands.

Sure enough, Pepys (or Pepys's) Island is marked on some charts of the era, but subsequent exploration over the next century failed to find any trace of it. Some say it was all an invention, to avoid returning home with no discoveries to show off. In 1765 John Byron 'coasted the islands for 70 leagues and saw no evidence of anyone being there'.

Or did Cowley simply get the co-ordinates wrong? The same name has been taken to apply to a perfectly real place 350 miles or so to the south, at about 54 degrees of latitude: South Georgia. If that name rings a bell then the chances are you first heard it in the context of the Falkland Islands and the 1982 war between Britain and Argentina. Probably not many people were even aware of the Falklands until then, much less able to place them on a map. If you can cast your mind back that far, you may have been puzzled to hear on the news of Argentinian scrap-metal merchants taking over an abandoned Norwegian whaling station on South Georgia. Eh? This seemed a strange reason for giving the British public the trouble of reaching down the atlas, but it was clearly being interpreted as the opening of hostilities. Supposedly these were not real scrap dealers at all but the advance party for an invasion.[90] A fortnight later, Argentine troops attacked and the die was cast.

Over the centuries the islands have had different owners and different names. The discoverer of the Falklands is often said to be Sebald de Weert of the Netherlands in 1600, though they had been sighted on various earlier occasions and appear on sixteenth-century charts, but the Dutch never claimed them as a possession. France was the first to take control, in 1764, challenged very shortly afterwards by the British.[91] In 1774 the islands were ceded to the Spanish, and after the demise of that

[90] In fact, for the last four years, the Argentinians had already been maintaining a presence a few hundred miles away in the South Sandwich Isles, no doubt testing the water, and no action had been taken by Britain.
[91] Ironic, perhaps, that the French should have been such staunch supporters of the British military action in 1982.

empire, Argentina took over in 1826. In 1833 a sort of power vacuum emerged, which the British promptly exploited to take a firm grip over 'these miserable islands', as Charles Darwin called them when his scientific ship the *Beagle* visited them shortly afterwards. Whatever the rights and wrongs of the matter, they have remained under British control ever since – give or take 72 days in 1982.

Various names may or may not have referred to the Falklands. In 1592 John Davis, commander of the *Desire*, was blown off course and sighted some undiscovered islands which became known as Davis's Land. Were they the Falklands? We are in kelp-clogged waters here. A couple of years later Richard Hawkins called by and gave them the rather more original name of 'Hawkins' Maidenland', seemingly a reference to the 'Virgin Queen' Elizabeth I. The Dutch name was the Sebald Islands (*Islas Sebaldinas* or *Sebaldes* in Spanish), after Sebald de Weert. But the most memorable must be the *Islas de Sansón y de los Patos* ('Islands of Samson and the Ducks'), found on Spanish charts of the early sixteenth century. John Strong, who had first landed in 1690, named the islands after his patron, the Fifth Viscount Falkland.

Today this is one of those places you can't even mention without taking sides. The Americans, officially neutral during the conflict, play it safe with 'Falkland Islands (Islas Malvinas)'. In Argentina, not to use the name Malvinas is a provocative act, and since the conflict everything from airports to municipalities to a sports stadium has been named or renamed accordingly; conversely to call them the Malvinas in English is to make quite a strong political statement. Yet for all its patriotically Argentinian flavour, this word Malvinas is actually just a Spanish adaptation of 'les Îles Malouines', the name coined in the eighteenth century by French sailors to commemorate a Breton port (Saint-Malo) named after a British saint (Maclovius or Machutus) who was probably born in Wales.

Georgetown

Ah, but which one? The second city of Gambia was called Georgetown, on an island in the River Gambia. It's now known as Janjanbureh. Es Castell on Minorca, the most easterly village in Spain, was originally called Georgetown after George III; the Spanish renamed it Villacarlos after Carlos III, but the locals call it after the nearby fort (*castell*) of San Felip.

However, many Georgetowns are still with us. The capital of Ascension Island is Georgetown, as is that of Guyana.[92] It's a popular place name in the Caribbean: Grenada has its Georgetown, likewise Saint Vincent and the Grenadines; the capital of the British Overseas Territory of the Cayman Islands is George Town, and there's another one tucked away somewhere in the Bahamas. Yet another George Town[93] is capital of the Malaysian state of Penang. There's a Georgetown on Prince Edward Island,[94] and a tiny village of the same name in Newfoundland and Labrador. Georgetown is both a district of Allahabad in Uttar Pradesh[95] and an area of Tredegar, South Wales.

American Georgetowns can be found in California, Colorado, Connecticut, Delaware, Florida, Georgia, Idaho, Illinois, Kentucky, Mississippi, Ohio, South Carolina and

[92] It was Longchamps or Nouvelle Ville under the French, then briefly Stabroek under the Dutch (after Nicolaas Geelvinck, Lord of Stabroek, President of the Dutch West India Company), before becoming Georgetown on 29 April 1812 in honour of King George III.

[93] It was founded in 1786 as Fort Cornwallis after Charles Cornwallis, 1st Marquis and 2nd Earl Cornwallis, Governor-General of India (1786–93 and 1805), and renamed after King George III, or was it his son, Prince George Augustus Frederick, who became King George IV in 1820?

[94] Named in 1765 after King George III.

Texas. And so on, and so on. Don't let's even start on all the Fort Georges out there, not to mention George Land and Georgia and a few places simply called George.[96]

Of course, George has been one of the most popular names of British kings. There are also plenty of Jamestowns and Charlesto(w)ns, not to mention North and South Carolina.[97] Before you deride the lack of originality of the explorers and colonial adventurers of yesteryear, spare a thought for the pressures they must have felt themselves under to please the sponsor. Whether you're a king, a minister or just a wealthy capitalist, if you put up the money to send an expedition halfway round the world, the least you can expect in return is for them to scatter your name around the map a bit. It seems only polite.

[95] Georgetown seems to have escaped the Indian renaming frenzy, though Allahabad may soon become Prayag.

[96] Western Australia, Québec, South Africa and Indiana, USA.

[97] Originally after the French King Charles IX (1550–74), in Latin *Carolus*.

Piddle

The River Piddle rises in the Dorset village of Alton Pancras, formerly known as Awultune, Anglo-Saxon for 'settlement at the source of the river'. The name Piddle means a marsh or fen in Anglo-Saxon. It's also known as the Trent (not to be confused with the more famous one further north), which is one of a number of river names, such as Avon, Esk, Tyne and Ouse, that simply mean 'river' or 'water'. There is a Wyre Piddle in Worcestershire, named after the Wyre forest, which may be from a Celtic river-name meaning 'winding river'. But don't go jumping to conclusions about where the more familiar sense of piddle comes from: according to the *Oxford English Dictionary* it may be a euphemism for 'piss' but the origin is uncertain and no connection with flowing streams is suggested.

The river passes through places with names like Piddlehinton and Piddletrenthide, but also Puddletown, Briantspuddle and Turnerspuddle. Yes, somewhere along the line the piddle turned into a puddle. For example, Affpiddle, mentioned in the Domesday Book in 1086 as Affapidela ('Estate on the River Piddle of a man called Æffa'), is now known as Affpuddle. The same thing happened to the rather more famous Tolpuddle, where the 'Martyrs'[98] came from: it appears in the Domesday Book as Pidele, becoming Tollepidele in 1210.

Some say this bowdlerisation happened at the time of a visit to the area by Queen Victoria, but it's rather unfair that her

---

[98] They founded the Friendly Society of Agricultural Labourers in 1834, were convicted under an obscure law of swearing a secret oath of loyalty to each other, and transported to Australia.

name has come to symbolise anything stuffy or prudish, such as the myth that even legs of pianos had to be shrouded in cloth to prevent impropriety. If she had known how she would be pictured by future generations she would probably have puddled herself laughing.

Biafra

The word Biafra (or Biafara or Biafar) has been used since the sixteenth century to refer to a wide area of West Africa, east of River Niger, extending down through Cameroon and into Gabon. In the modern world it is a southeastern region of Nigeria, which hit the headlines with a bang in 1967 when it unilaterally declared independence from the federal government. Over the next three years Biafra became a kind of synonym for war and suffering witnessed in all its horror by ordinary people in the West from the comfort of their own homes – the world's first media famine.

Nigeria gained its independence from Britain in 1960. It had always been a patchwork of different nations and kingdoms, one of the richest parts of Africa but dogged by autocratic military government and riven by ethnic conflict, something economists tell us can act as a brake on economic growth and development. There are hundreds of ethnic groups, speaking something like 500 languages between them. However, about two thirds of the population belong to one of four main nationalities: the Yoruba of the southwest, the Muslim Hausa and Fulani in the north, and the Igbo, a Christian people in the oil-rich southeast.

In January 1966 Igbo army officers launched an unsuccessful coup. The result was bloody reprisals against ethnic Igbo living in the north, where up to 30,000 Igbos were killed in ethnic conflict with Hausas, which some claimed amounted to genocide. On 30 May 1967 the head of the Eastern Region, Lieutenant Colonel Emeka Ojukwu, unilaterally declared the independent Republic of Biafra.

Biafran independence was recognised by only five countries, but government papers released recently prove that

France, which officially denied any involvement, had the opposite aim and was in fact supplying quantities of arms to the Biafrans via Gabon and the Ivory Coast. French influence in West Africa, though strong, could only benefit from the break-up of Nigeria, the ex-British local superpower. The Soviet Union, too, saw its chance to increase its influence in the area in the event of a political shake-up. South Africa, Rhodesia and Portugal (which still controlled the nearby islands of São Tomé and Príncipe) also came to the aid of the new state. But, worried by the thought of political instability

and the threat to oil supplies, in which it had major holdings, Britain chose to back the federal government.

So the weapons flooded in, and a brutal civil war raged. After initial advances, the Biafran forces were pushed back steadily. The federal government imposed a blockade and the result was mass starvation, on a scale hard to conceive even today in these days of global rolling news and compassion fatigue. The fighting and famine cost the lives of anything up to a million people. Western photographers such as Don McCullin introduced the world to the sight of children with stick-thin limbs and the grotesquely distended stomachs characteristic of protein deficiency, images which have since become all too familiar in subsequent decades.

So much so that, forty years on, the name of Biafra never seems to be heard. The American punk rocker Eric Reed Boucher, former lead singer of the Dead Kennedys, uses the stage name Jello Biafra, 'ironically' juxtaposing the concepts of mass starvation in Africa and the nutritionally worthless junk food of the West (Jell-O is American for jelly) in order to, oh, you know, shock us all out of our complacency, or whatever. Obtuse? Obscene? Otiose, now that Biafra is largely forgotten? Up to you.

United States of Belgium

The last fifty years have seen Benelux, the European Coal and Steel Community, the Common Market, the European Economic Community and the European Union, to name but a few stages in the pan-European project. There is often talk of a 'United States of Europe' as the ultimate destination. Not so widely known is the fact that there was once a United States of Belgium, also known as the United Belgian (or Belgium) States or United Netherlands States.

This history of the Low Countries is a complicated affair. The area in question may be small, but it has been fought over not only by the neighbouring powers of France and what is now Germany, but also by the Austrian Habsburg Empire. In the 1780s, at a time when some of Europe was struggling to throw off the old dynastic empires and establish republics, the Emperor Joseph II was trying to centralise power in Vienna; and in January 1789 discontented elements in Brabant[99] disowned the supremacy of the Habsburgs. The rest of the Austrian Netherlands, except Luxembourg, joined in what became known as the Brabant Revolution, as did revolutionaries in the Prince-Bishopric of Liège,[100] then an independent entity within the Habsburg Empire, and a treaty was signed establishing the Verenigde Nederlandse Staten or États-Belgiques-Unis on the model of the American Declaration of Independence of 1776. The United States of Belgium[101] was born.

[99] Whose colours of black, yellow and red are still those of the nation of Belgium.
[100] Then spelled Liége.
[101] There had never been such a country as 'Belgium', so where did the name come from? Another thing the Romans did for us. When in 57 BC Julius Caesar added these northern regions to the province of Gaul, he named them *Gallia Belgica* after a local Celtic tribe, the *Belgae*.

However, united was one thing the new state was not. Disagreements between the so-called Statist movement and their rivals the Vonckists weakened their alliance and allowed the Austrians to regain control before the year was out. They in turn were taken over by the French Republic in 1795, and Belgium would have to wait until 1830 to become a sovereign state again.

But a new concept had been born: Belgium. Plucky little Belgium, the cockpit of Europe. The victim of the evil Hun in the First World War, trampled underfoot again in the Second. It is a small, little-known and often overlooked country,[102] over which not only tanks have rolled on the way to more important places but tourist coaches too; in the title of the 1969 film comedy, *If It's Tuesday, This Must Be Belgium*. But allowing for its recent birth and small size, it surely has as much to offer as anywhere else on the continent. What a shame it is known mainly in Britain as the home of Hercule Poirot, bureaucracy and *moules frites* – and as the favourite swearword of Zaphod Beeblebrox.[103]

---

[102] Actually, what is the smallest country in Europe? It's a philosophical rather than a factual question. Forget all those improbably tiny microstates, entertaining though they are. What is the smallest *proper* country, one with a proper government and an army and a university and so on? Is it Belgium?

[103] According to Douglas Adams's classic space fantasy *The Hitchhiker's Guide to the Galaxy*, 'On Earth, Belgium refers to a small country. Throughout the rest of the galaxy, Belgium is the most unspeakably rude word there is.'

New Hebrides

These eighty-odd islands in the southwest Pacific, about a thousand miles east of Australia, were 'discovered' by the Portuguese explorer Pedro Fernandes de Queirós in 1606. Looking for the fabled great southern continent, Terra Australis, he landed on an island he called Austrália del Espíritu Santo. Having named it after the Holy Spirit, he must have gone on his way without any Caledonian resemblances occurring to him, as too did the Frenchman Louis-Antoine de Bougainville in 1768. Captain Cook arrived in 1774, and it is apparently to him we owe this somewhat incongruous name. Did something in the rustling of the palm fronds suggest to him the skirl of the pipes? Was it perhaps the tanned natives, active volcanoes and endless stretches of sun-kissed sand that recalled the Western Isles of Scotland?[104] We may never know.

Britain and France vied for supremacy in the islands until eventually in 1906 a condominium was established whereby the New Hebrides, or Nouvelles-Hébrides, would be ruled by both powers in separate English-speaking and French-speaking communities: a cumbersome arrangement certainly, and one that is still considered an obstacle to unity. As well as the two colonial languages there are over a hundred local ones, which makes this small archipelago one of the most linguistically rich places in the world. In such situations a lingua franca tends to emerge whenever people travel outside their immediate area or are thrown together with speakers of other tongues. In this case it's Bislama, or Beach-la-Mar as it used to be called, and it's the third official language of what is

[104] Incidentally, the name of the original Hebrides is said to have originated in a misreading of the Latin *Hebudes* – but that need not detain us here.

now, since independence in 1980, the Republic of Vanuatu.

Bislama is basically a mixture of English words with Melanesian grammar – not strictly speaking a pidgin but a creole, since it's spoken as a first language in the two largest cities, Port Vila and Luganville. It's unusual among languages in being named after a marine invertebrate: the sea cucumber or trepang (*bêche de mer* in French, from Portuguese *bicho do mar*). These primitive plankton-eaters with their gelatinous bodies and leathery skins may seem unappealing but in dried form they are a great delicacy in the Far East.

The religious make-up of the islands is just as complex as the linguistic situation. Most islanders consider themselves Christians, with Presbyterians and Anglicans accounting for nearly half the observant population and Catholics not much more than 10 per cent; the rest is made up of a diverse assortment of denominations from Seventh-Day Adventists to something called the Neil Thomas Ministries. A significant minority still holds to indigenous beliefs, known as *kastom* (custom), which far from being stamped out by the European missionaries have experienced something of a revival since independence, partly as a consequence of the massive, disorientating culture shock that can happen when the old and new worlds collide head-on. One of the stranger manifestations of this is what anthropologists call 'cargo cults', a form of millenarianism – or to less sympathetic observers, a form of madness.

Such cults have been observed since the early years of the twentieth century, when the modern world was beginning to make itself felt in the remotest places with unsettling and bewildering effects on the belief systems of tribal peoples. They sprang into sharp relief with the arrival of American troops in the New Hebrides during the Second World War, when the mental world of the islanders was turned upside down by the arrival of planeloads of 'cargo' – desirable consumer goods and comestibles. Were these the chariots of the gods? Where had all this lovely stuff been hiding over the centuries, and how could they keep it coming?

Probably the best-known and most durable cult is that of 'John Frum'. In the highly syncretic nature of religion in these parts, Christianity and *kastom* get mixed and matched and rolled up together; the mystical figure of John Frum serves as the embodiment of the Western cornucopia, a kind of amalgam of Jesus, John the Baptist and Father Christmas, and he lives in a volcano. No one knows whether there once was a real person of that name or whether it is in fact a shortening of 'John from America'. The colonial authorities clamped down hard on this movement, with its rebellious attitude (there was even an attempt to secede from the condominium in 1974), its materialism and its revaluation of traditional beliefs and practices. The islanders started to feel that they had got very little from the missionaries and colonists; on the other hand, the American troops and their 'cargo' were the object of a quasi-religious devotion.

By the time the Americans left, the war in the Pacific over, they had stockpiled more assorted stuff than they knew what to do with. So, at a place now nicknamed Million Dollar Point, they simply bulldozed into the sea vast piles of surplus equipment and supplies. Vehicles, uniforms, cases of Coca-Cola: what could not be drowned was buried or burned, for reasons that are still not completely clear.

The islanders must have struggled to understand such wanton destruction. And no new consignments were arriving. Perhaps by re-creating the conditions under which the cargo had arrived, they could make the magic happen again. Imitation airstrips were built in the jungle, complete with control tower, bamboo aerials and coconut-shell headphones to draw the good stuff down from the skies. The red cross, as seen on ambulances and medical supplies, became the symbol of the cult. To this day, every 15 February, villagers parade with wooden 'rifles', the letters USA painted on their chests. The John Frum movement is also a political party with two MPs.

On the island of Tanna, one of the more traditional parts of Vanuatu, things took what seem to us Westerners a particularly bizarre turn. You may have heard it said that Prince Philip, our own dear Duke of Edinburgh, is worshipped there as a god. Supposedly the village of Yaohnanen once sent him a royal gift of a ceremonial club or *nalnal*, and HRH reciprocated with a signed photograph of himself, which is a kind of holy relic for some of the villagers. He is their John Frum.

Something rather similar happened in 1960s Papua New Guinea with US President Lyndon B Johnson. The population of the island of New Hanover voted massively for him in the local elections, even though of course he was never actually a candidate.[105] Whether or not the islanders actually thought he would come and save them with his American know-how and doubtless some nice cargo, a substantial sum of money was supposedly offered him in return for his services as King of New Hanover. In the darker moments of his presidency, with race riots, a thousand American soldiers dying in Vietnam every month and protesters chanting about how many kids he had killed today, LBJ must surely have been tempted.

---

[105] He also had a town named after him in Malaysia, but that's another story altogether.

Carnarvon

It's still Carnarvon in Western Australia and the Northern Cape Province of South Africa, and it was the Fifth Earl of Carnarvon who bankrolled the excavation of Tutankhamun's tomb in 1923. But in Wales, it's more familiar as Caernarvon, or now that the native Welsh name is official, Caernarfon, since there is no v in modern Welsh spelling. The *caer* part, like English 'chester', comes from the Latin *castrum*, meaning a fortified town of the sort the Romans built so many of around Britain. Segontium was built about AD 75 by Agricola, and connected by a Roman road to the base at Chester[106] itself. But whereas the Latin name probably refers to the River Seiont that the fort overlooks, which is probably to do with the British tribe of the *Segontiaci*, the Welsh one means the fort in the district of Arfon: *Caer yn Arfon*. Arfon is the place 'opposite Anglesey', *ar Fôn*. Anglesey is *Môn*[107] in Welsh, *Mona* in Latin.[108] So perhaps the English name should really be Angleseychester, or more elegantly, if confusingly for the tourists, Monchester.

---

[106] In Welsh, *Caer*.
[107] In certain contexts the initial changes to f (still pronounced v), hence Ynys Môn, the isle of Anglesey, but Sir Fôn, the county of Anglesey.
[108] A name also sometimes applied to the Isle of Man.

Senegambia

We in the West, or so it often seems, are living in a world dominated by the quest for elusive commodities like novelty and variety. Many of us are also in search of something called identity – 'roots', if you like. In order to satisfy these urges, in order to find not only new places and experiences but 'ourselves', we travel. Having explored, colonised and exploited much of the world over the last few centuries, we are now sending out armies of tourists to do the same in the name of (let us hope) peace and prosperity. Places that only a few years ago were famous for all the wrong reasons – Vietnam, Ethiopia, Georgia – are now almost mainstream holiday destinations. Others, such as Yugoslavia, Lebanon and Iraq, have recently moved in the other direction, but among their very best hopes for political stability and long-term economic success is surely tourism.

Thus it is that many British people have heard of, or even visited, a tiny West African country called the Gambia – or just 'Gambia', since it's one of those places like (the) Ukraine and (the) Lebanon where the definite article is tending to fall out of use.[109]

As mainland states go, Gambia is what you might call compact and bijou; with a land area of less than 4,500 square miles it ranks somewhere between Qatar and Montenegro and is the smallest country on the African continent. It's also one of the world's more unusually shaped states, entirely enclosed (but for a few miles of coastline) by Senegal, and for most of its length simply lining the banks of the River Gambia, which runs west for 700 miles from the Fouta

[109] However, for some reason we still call it The Hague.

Djallon plateau in Guinea into the Atlantic Ocean. At the rivermouth is St Mary's Island, which is the site of the Gambian capital, founded in 1816 as Bathurst[110] and known since 1973 as Banjul.

While still mainly an agricultural country dependent on groundnut[111] farming, Gambia has plenty going for it as a holiday destination. As well as lounging on beaches and taking trips upriver, the tourist with a sense of history can visit UNESCO-listed World Heritage Sites such as James Island,[112] a British trading post for gold, ivory and slaves, and the eighth-century stone circles near Janjanbureh (formerly Georgetown).

Gambia has a long and complex colonial history. Part of the Manding Empire of Mali since the fourteenth century, it was claimed by the Portuguese only to be sold on to Britain,

[110] After Henry Bathurst, Secretary of State for War and the Colonies from 1812 to 1827.
[111] Peanuts, as we prefer to call them here.
[112] Named after the then Duke of York, later King James II.

having been briefly and perhaps somewhat bizarrely a possession of the Polish-Lithuanian Commonwealth. What perhaps looks like a strange, artificially shaped sort of a country is in fact due to a surprisingly old geopolitical fault line based on colonial rivalry: while the British had long held control of the river, the surrounding areas of French influence had prevented them expanding outwards from it. The present borders were established in 1889 by agreement with France, the colonial rulers of Senegal, and Gambia achieved independence in 1965.

Since then it has naturally had a very close relationship with the country that enfolds it like the bread around a hot dog. So much so that the two countries actually reached a sort of merger agreement in 1981. The result was the Senegambia Confederation of 1982, which involved not only economic and monetary union and the integration of foreign policies and security forces, but a confederate parliament. Naturally, as the larger partner, Senegal was to have a dominant part to play in all this, controlling the confederal presidency and two thirds of the parliament, and this failed to play well in the smaller nation. When the Gambia refused to move closer towards union, the infant confederation was dissolved by Senegal on 30 September 1989.

However, the name Senegambia[113] goes back way before the 1980s. Like so many approximate geographical terms that have since come to be the names of specific modern states, it had been in use long since to refer to this important area of West Africa, and it was the name of the British colony from 1765. Its importance was not only economic but strategic, first as a slave port and then, after slavery was outlawed under British law in 1807, as a base for controlling the slave trade that continued to flourish clandestinely.

In the United States, as late as the mid-twentieth century, the term Senegambian was still used to mean a black American, or African-American to use the preferred term of

[113] A felicitous choice you might think much better than Gambegal.

today. In 1943 the *Pittsburgh Courier* used it thus, seemingly without negative connotations: 'There are thousands of Negroes living in similar or better houses, despite the race hustling talk about the "horrible houses" of Harlem. All the civilized Senegambians live in good homes.'

Thus the name Gambia may have been more widely known in America than Britain, especially after the publication of *Roots: The Saga of an American Family*, Alex Haley's Pulitzer-Prize-winning novel of 1976, which went on to become a television series and indeed to foster an entire industry of black Americans tracing their family origins to West Africa. Although the book was intended as fiction, Haley did claim to have researched his story extensively, and to have found sources in Africa confirming that his hero Kunta Kinte, taken as a slave from the Gambian village of Juffure on the north bank of the river in 1767, had really existed and was his ancestor. A folk memory in his family of the words 'Kamby Bolongo' (Gambia River) had led him there.

The question of the book's authenticity has since been the subject of much doubt, or least vigorous debate. But whatever the truth of the matter – and it seems generally accepted as unlikely that Haley really managed to trace his ancestry back through the centuries of slavery to a particular Gambian village where a folk memory of his family still existed – the book captured the imaginations of thousands of Americans of all races, and, be it said without wishing to seem cynical, did wonders for the nascent tourist trade of Gambia.

A different and even more debatable question is what wonders it may have done for the consciousness of Black Americans. Did it encourage them to believe unrealistic and divisive fantasies of their Africanness,[114] likely to be shattered

---

[114] The African intelligentsia had a word for it – negritude, a literary and political movement originating in the 1930s, which emphasised the shared black heritage of the African diaspora.

when they arrived in the real Africa with their dollars and their First World attitudes, hoping to bond with Africans who might be their distant relatives, only to be treated as just another sort of white folks? Or did it give the denizens of the Melting Pot that commodity far more precious in our anonymous modern world than all the gold and ivory exported in the past – roots?[115]

---

[115] Apparently, though this is hardly relevant, the Gambia also offers an emergency landing site for NASA space shuttles at Yundum International Airport.

The Islands of Saint Ursula and the Eleven Thousand Virgins

This, or rather *Santa Ursula y las Once Mil Vírgenes*, is the fanciful name that came to the mind of Christopher Columbus when in 1493 he sighted a group of about 90 islands in the Caribbean, at the eastern extremity of the Greater Antilles. It was 21 October, the feast of St Ursula, a somewhat historically dubious fourth-century virgin and martyr. Today the islands are divided between British and US administration and known more simply as the Virgin Islands.

They are a sadly typical story of colonial rapacity: settled by British and Spanish planters, their native Amerindian population decimated, they became a centre for the highly profitable sugar trade, using slave labour imported from Africa on the notorious 'Triangular Trade'[116] until eventually demand for sugar cane waned as sugar beet began to be cultivated in Europe and America. They were also an important strategic possession in these famously piratical waters, and there was much jockeying for position between various colonial powers. In 1733 Denmark actually bought their Danish West Indies from the French, but in 1917 sold them on again for 25 million dollars to the United States, which still controls the majority of the islands (about sixty) as an 'unincorporated territory'. The British possessions (about forty islands) were part of the colony of the Leeward Islands till 1956, before becoming

---

[116] Sugar to New England or Britain; rum, weapons and assorted dry goods from there to Africa; then back to the Caribbean with more slaves.

autonomous in 1967. After a long history of brutality and exploitation, the islands have finally achieved a more peaceful prosperity through not only tourism but also financial services.

The emblem of the Virgin Islands is, naturally, St Ursula, depicted with an oil lamp and eleven others for her squad of virgins. But who was this Ursula?

According to the *Passio XI. MM. SS. Virginum,* supposedly based on the revelations made about a thousand years ago to one Helentrude, a nun from near Paderborn in Germany, Ursula was the beautiful daughter of the (probably mythical) British King Donatus or Deonotus of Dumnonia in the southwest of England. A local pagan prince demanded her hand in marriage, an ever-present risk for female saints in those days, but thanks to a warning dream, she demanded a three-year sabbatical in order to go on a

pilgrimage to Rome. She took some companions with her and, being a royal personage, her retinue was large: 11,000 virgins. As Butler's *Lives of the Saints* puts it, 'Ursula was the conductor and encourager of the holy troop'. They sailed to Germany in eleven ships – large ones presumably – up the Rhine to Cologne and Basel. Then, being 11,000 healthy, vigorous young women, they continued to Rome on foot. Pope Cyriacus[117] gave them his blessing and a military escort for the return journey, which came in handy when the party was

---

[117] Who probably never existed either.

attacked by the Huns near Cologne. Attila was very taken with Ursula and offered to spare her life if she would marry him, but of course she quite properly refused and was put to death.

You will be shocked and saddened to hear that the credibility of this uplifting tale has been doubted since the thirteenth century, especially the bit about Attila. In fact in 1969, as part of a clean-up of some of the more absurd and disreputable cults, Ursula was removed from the general calendar of saints recognised by the Catholic Church. First martyred, then struck off – and by your own side! The cynics would even have us believe that the whole business of 11,000 virgins is in fact a misreading of the name of one of Ursula's companions, Undecimilla, as *undecim millia* (11,000); or that the abbreviation 'XI. M. V.' for eleven martyred virgins[118] was misunderstood as the Roman numerals for 11,000.

Some people are no fun.

[118] Their names, incidentally, were Britula, Gregoria, Martha, Palladia, Pinnosa, Rabacia, Saturia, Saturnina, Saula, Sencia and Ursula.

Skildar

Even the name of this place is a matter of legend and conjecture. Skildar is how the remote island group we now call Saint Kilda was identified on a sixteenth-century map, and supposedly this came to be misinterpreted as 'S. Kilda'. The thing everyone agrees on is that there is no such saint as Kilda and never was, and anyway that name was probably not meant to refer to the islands in question (Hirta and its satellites Soay and Boreray). Skildar means 'shields' in Norse,[119] referring to the shape of the landmass – but in fact St Kilda is mountainous and jagged, so the label may have accidentally transferred itself from a low-lying island nearer the mainland. That's one theory at least. According to the seventeenth-century antiquarian Martin Martin,[120] the name 'is taken from one Kilder, who lived here; and from him the large well Toubir-Kilda ['Childa's Well' in Gaelic] has also its name'. Or is it perhaps from the Norse *sunt kelda*, meaning 'sweet well-water'? Who knows?

St Kilda is a truly remote place: over a hundred miles from the mainland of Scotland, 'on the margine of the world' according to the fourteenth-century chronicler John of Fordun. It had one not very good harbour, fierce storms battered the island from September to April, and until a radio station was installed in 1913, there was no reliable means of communication with the outside world. And yet this inhospitable outpost appears to have been more or less successfully inhabited for thousands of years, until the modern era proved too much for it.

[119] The language of St Kilda from the ninth to the fifteenth centuries.
[120] *A Description of the Western Islands of Scotland* (1703).

The volcanic crags of St Kilda are said to be the highest in Europe, rising to 1,400 feet, and the men of St Kilda used to jump about them like goats in order to harvest the seabirds and eggs that provided both the mainstay of their diet and their rent to the landlords, the McLeods of Harris and Skye. These people apparently thought nothing of being lowered over a precipice, carrying a sheep, just to get the benefit of a few square feet of extra grazing on a grassy ledge. In fact, climbing skills were assessed as a measure of manhood: supposedly a St Kildan youth could not marry until he had proved his skill by balancing on one foot on the Mistress Stone, a natural stone arch over a 250-foot drop. The sheep in question are the archaic Soay sheep,[121] rather like the Mediterranean mouflon, thought to have arrived on the island in the Bronze Age. They naturally shed their wool, which the St Kildans simply pulled off rather than using shears. Soay, from the Old Norse, actually means Sheep Island. It's not the only creature unique to the place: isolated from mainland influences for so long, several distinct subspecies evolved, most famously the St Kilda wren.[122]

In 1898 the naturalist Richard Kearton spent some time on St Kilda and got to know the locals well. 'For nine months in the year,' he reported in his book *With Nature and a Camera*, 'the inhabitants of St Kilda are doomed to an utter ignorance of the doings of the outer world unless some stray fishing smack should, under favourable conditions of wind and tide, venture to drop in and see them.'

Part of the folklore surrounding the place is that if an urgent message needed to be got to the mainland, the only way was to send it by the so-called 'St Kilda Mailboat', which consisted of a bladder for buoyancy, trailing a small wooden box containing the message, with a penny for a stamp and a note requesting the finder to put the letter in the post. Apparently,

---

[121] *Ovis aries*, if you are a sheep-fancier, and of course no one is implying anything unsavoury by that.
[122] *Troglodytes troglodytes hirtensis*, for those who prefer birds to sheep.

this version of the message-in-a-bottle worked surprisingly well when the wind and sea were right.

Another picture of the isolation of the St Kildans, mental as well as physical, is given by the story of a woman who was part of a group that travelled to the island of Harris. The boat was blown off course and landed on an unfamiliar part of the coast. As the group searched for human habitation, she got separated from the others and came across a strange tall tower. The door was open; she wandered inside and up a spiral staircase, at the top of which she saw a bearded man surrounded by a blaze of light. Naturally, she fell on her knees and praised the Almighty. The lighthouse keeper, for his part, thought this delirious hag who had appeared out of nowhere must be a witch and was equally terrified.[123]

It's hard to resist the cliché, and indeed it seems fair to say that life on St Kilda really had not changed much for many generations until the nineteenth century. Then, something we now call tourism started to happen. Not just the occasional gentleman traveller calling by, but whole steamer-loads of day-trippers coming to gawp at the deliciously primitive inhabitants of this forgotten corner of Britain. Whether one saw St Kilda as a prelapsarian paradise sequestered from the clangour of modern life, or as a grotesque rabble of throwbacks subsisting on the margins of civilisation, whether the St Kildans were noble savages or village idiots, what could be more titillating to romantic Victorian sensibilities?

Like tourists anywhere, they brought with them money and a desire to buy souvenirs, and they gradually distorted the island's subsistence economy until it became dependent on the 'steamer season' – exactly what has since happened, and is still happening, in many parts of the Third World. Just as importantly, the visitors brought a flavour of the outside world and what it might be like to live in a place where you could not

---

[123] The same superstition is quoted as the reason for the killing in 1840 of what is believed to have been the last great auk in the British Isles, killed by fowlers on Stac an Armin. It was a witch and they blamed it for calling up a storm, as witches are known to do when riled.

only feed yourself but earn money, travel as you wished, and perhaps even marry someone you hadn't known since infancy.

Long famed for their hospitality, which is perhaps really a kind of survival instinct among people living in such marginal environments, the St Kildans began to be seen as greedy and acquisitive, a sort of rural street urchin who would aggressively demand a tip for the slightest service. And yet, according to anecdote, they retained a kind of childlike innocence that could be both touching and tragic. Though the heavy hand of fundamentalist theology had stamped out whatever frivolous instincts previously existed among them, dancing and music and so on being the work of the devil, they adored sweets. The story is also told of a woman so fascinated to see an orange for the first time that she took it in payment for a bale of tweed – her entire year's work. The orange was installed in a place of honour on the windowsill where it stayed until it rotted.

As the nineteenth century drew to its close, the population of St Kilda had dropped steadily, partly though infections brought in by visitors.[124] In 1920 there were 73 people left on the island; eight years later, just 37 remained, and fiercely as they loved their island, the St Kildans wondered how long it was realistic to hang on there. In 1930 they officially petitioned the British Government to evacuate them.[125] They could hardly rebuild St Kilda in exile: their whole way of life had ceased to exist. Many ended up in Australia, where, coincidentally, there is a suburb of Melbourne named St Kilda.[126]

---

[124] There was also an endemic problem with infant tetanus, which turned out to be caused by the custom of sealing the umbilical scar of newborns with fulmar oil.

[125] A similar evacuation had already taken place on Mingulay, sometimes referred to as 'the near St Kilda', at the southernmost tip of the Outer Hebrides, in 1911.

[126] After *The Lady of St Kilda*, a schooner that visited the seven-year-old township of Melbourne in 1842, and whose name commemorated an early tourist trip to the islands by her owner, Sir Thomas Dyke Acland, and his wife. Confusingly, there is also a suburb of Adelaide called St Kilda, and another St Kilda in New Zealand.

Since the evacuation Hirta has been used as a radar tracking station for the missile firing range on Benbecula, and the only people living there now are either military personnel or staff and volunteers working for the National Trust for Scotland. The St Kilda subspecies of the house mouse, *Mus musculus muralis*, is extinct.

South West Africa

It's not only natural geographical features and ethnic differences that account for the twists and turns of borders: political considerations make funny shapes on the map. Get out that atlas, if you haven't done so already, and turn up South West Africa – the name tells you where to look for it, though if your atlas is up to date it will be called Namibia. It must surely be a strong candidate for strangest-shaped country in the world. Jutting out from the northeast corner is a strange phallic protrusion some 280 miles long and about twenty miles wide. It looks a bit like what geologists call an igneous intrusion, a seam of molten rock running along a fault line, the line in question being the border between Botswana and Angola.[127] To pursue the analogy, when the magma reaches the harder 'country rock'[128] where Zambia, Zimbabwe and Botswana meet, it comes to a halt and pools in a triangular blob between the Cuando, Chobe and Zambezi Rivers. Fifty miles to the west lies the Okavango Delta, where the Okavango sinks into the Kalahari sands, its way to the sea thwarted by a tectonic uplift. Thus, Namibia has borders not only with Angola, Botswana and South Africa, but also Zambia and Zimbabwe, which at first glance seem miles away.

The name of this strange protrusion is the Caprivi Strip.[129] It takes its name from the German Chancellor Leo von Caprivi,[130]

[127] In America it would be called a panhandle. There's a very impressive one in Fairfield County, Connecticut, known as the Oblong, which results from territorial disputes in the seventeenth century. Just as well, because what passes for an appendage in Florida is about as phallic as the Mull of Kintyre.
[128] Remember we're talking geology not music here.
[129] It sounds even better in German: *Caprivizipfel*.
[130] Bismarck's successor.

who in 1890 obtained the territory for what was then German West Africa in an exchange with Britain. We have already mentioned the Heligoland–Zanzibar Treaty or *Helgoland–Sansibar Vertrag*, under which (among other things) Germany gave up Zanzibar in exchange for Heligoland and this crucial strip of territory, whose purpose was to give them access to the Zambezi and thence to German East Africa, also known as Tanganyika.

The Caprivi Strip has retained a strategic significance long after the era of German South West Africa. It served as a base for the ANC in their operations against the apartheid governments of South Africa, as well as for guerrillas in the civil wars of Angola and Rhodesia. Naturally, such artificially drawn borders often create problems on the ground when they divide those who feel themselves to be one nation with others across the border, and in the 1990s a Caprivi liberation movement was active. It was firmly put down by the Namibian government.

Until 1994 the country had an even stranger shape. A tiny exclave of South Africa dented its coastline at a port called Walvis Bay.[131] Like many places it was discovered but not colonised by the Portuguese, specifically Bartholomew Dias, who named it the *Golfo de Santa Maria da Conceição* ('Gulf of Saint Mary of the Conception'). The British seized it in 1878, aware of its strategic value, and incorporated it into the Cape Colony. Thus the Germans had to build their own Atlantic port, which they did in 1892 at a place called Tsoakhaub, Germanised as Swachaub. The original name supposedly means an opening of bowels, referring to the filthy appearance of the swirling, muddy floodwaters. In Afrikaans the city is known as Swakopmund ('the mouth of the Swakop'), and apart from fine beaches it offers one of the world's best-preserved examples of German colonial architecture. It is one of the very few places outside Europe where a significant minority of the population speaks German – getting on for a

---

[131] 'Whale Bay' in Afrikaans (*Walvisbaai*) and German (*Walfischbai*).

century after South West Africa ceased to be a German possession. Under the Treaty of Versailles after the First World War it was made a League of Nations Mandate, to be administered by South Africa, but things did not progress as planned. So far from fostering the country's progress to independence, the South Africans annexed Walvis Bay and treated the rest of the country as pretty much their own. Only after years of guerrilla warfare led by SWAPO, the South West Africa People's Organisation, did Namibia finally achieve its independence in 1990, and not until four years later did South Africa finally return Walvis Bay.

Namibia is a place of stark extremes: very rich in mineral deposits, it has five times the per capita GDP of some African countries, yet most of the population are unemployed and live in poverty. Mining makes up 20 per cent of GDP: copper, lead, tin, zinc, silver, tungsten and uranium as well as the famous diamond mines.[132] But the majority of people are agriculturalists, farming the black Karakul sheep, a central Asian

---

[132] Security is naturally a prime concern where tiny pieces of carbon worth vast sums are mined by poor people. To make it harder to smuggle anything out, no vehicle that enters the compound is allowed to leave – ever. When finished with it must sit rusting in the sunshine until it disintegrates into the sand.

breed introduced in the early twentieth century by the German colonists.

This is one of the world's least densely populated countries, with fewer than seven people per square mile,[133] but it is surprisingly diverse. About 12 per cent of the population is white, the largest white minority anywhere south of the Sahara apart from South Africa; they are not only of German, Dutch and British ancestry but also Portuguese (in many cases immigrants from Angola) and French. About half of the population are members of the Ovambo nation, who migrated south from the upper Zambezi; the original Khoisan inhabitants, including the famous Bushmen (or San), make up about 3 per cent.

Even smaller in number, a few tens of thousands, are a remarkable group called the Rehoboth Basters,[134] who are the offspring of unions between Dutch settlers and African women, whose ancestors 'trekked' to South West Africa from the Cape Colony in 1868. In 1872 they founded the 'Free Republic of Rehoboth'. Rehoboth ('wide expanses') is the biblical name given to the place by German missionaries, and if the name Baster (or Baaster) makes you think of 'illegitimate' ancestry you would be right, since that is indeed the Dutch meaning. But the Basters wear the name with pride. They consider themselves different to other 'Coloureds', and cling to a conservative, Dutch, Calvinist, Afrikaans identity. But of course, to the apartheid regime they were still basically black, and were assigned a 'bantustan' or homeland just like any other non-white minority.

Other peoples have suffered even worse. The Herero people of Damaraland in north-central Namibia took part in a rebellion against the brutal colonial regime in 1904, in which Germans were killed and their farms laid waste. Fourteen thousand German troops were dispatched under General

---

[133] Britain has about a hundred times that density, and Hong Kong well over two thousand times.
[134] Despite their name, they are a 'group' in the sense of an ethnic minority not a popular music combo.

Lothar von Trotha who, signing himself 'the great General of the mighty German Emperor', declared that the Herero were no longer German subjects and that any found in German territory would be shot on sight. Tens of thousands died in the ensuing 'Herero Wars', including some 80 per cent of the Herero population. Others were driven into the Kalahari Desert or worked to death in concentration camps. Other tribes suffered a similar fate in what has been described as the first genocide of the twentieth century. In 2004, the centenary year, Germany officially accepted its historic and moral responsibility, but stopped short of paying the reparations for which the Herero recently sued both the German government and the Deutsche Bank.

Central Region

Central Region. Just listen to it. Allow the music of the words to caress your soul. Can you hear the distant sound of the pipes? Can you smell the peat smoke, taste the whisky? Feel the soft Scottish breeze ruffling your hair?

Alas, Central Region is no more. It had a brief life, from 1975 to 1996, barely achieving the age of majority before being brutally dismembered into Falkirk, Stirling and Clack-mannanshire. But who can say that around the hearth, from the bothies of Bonnybridge to the palaces of Polmont, they do not still tell tales of their lost domain: Central . . . Central . . . Central . . .?[135]

---

[135] However, no 'give us back our Central' movement has emerged to match the fervour with which the partisans of Rutland have reclaimed their homeland.

Fernando Pó

Not much is known about the fifteenth-century Portuguese explorer Fernão do Pó, but he lives on through the island that for five centuries bore his name: Fernando Pó or (for some reason) Fernando Póo. It was probably in 1472 that he sighted this tropical island in the Bight of Biafra,[136] 25 miles or so off the coast of Cameroon, but it was not called after him until 1494; he himself called it Formosa, the beautiful island, a name later and much more famously applied to what we now call Taiwan. This was not to be the last name-change by any means.

In 1778 Fernando Pó was ceded by Portugal to Spain, along with the territory of Río Muni (Mbini) 100 miles away on the mainland, a rare Spanish colonial presence in sub-Saharan Africa; however, the Spanish ruled it very much at arm's length, and from 1827 to 1858 the Royal Navy maintained a base there to control the traffic in human cargo along what was not for nothing called the Slave Coast. In 1834 a resident of the island argued passionately for its retention by the British on the grounds that 'slavers that are captured could in a few hours land the miserable beings with which they are freighted, but now, to increase their sufferings, they are sent to Sierra Leone; the casualties attending this passage, against generally adverse winds and currents, close stowage and stench, can be called nothing less than murder'.

Many freed slaves went on from Fernando Pó to start a new life in Liberia or Sierra Leone, but others settled where they had landed; a few thousand of their descendants, known as Fernandinos, still speak their own Afro-Portuguese creole,

---

[136] Also known as the Bight of Bonny.

also used by perhaps 70,000 Equatoguineans as a trading language. The island's existing population included a Bantu tribe called the Bubi, whose customs were documented with some interest by Europeans. Africa has long been famous for its talking drums, used to send messages from village to village. You may also have heard of whistled languages, which unlikely as it may seem still exist in a few places in the world;[137] shepherds in the mountains can communicate for miles by imitating the intonation of words. The Bubi used the same principle to talk to each other using a range of musical instruments.[138]

Not only was the island strategically important, it was profitable too. As well as timber and coffee, it was one of the first places in Africa to grow cocoa.[139] United with Río Muni as Spanish Guinea, it proved valuable in a different way: as a bolt hole for the German forces in Cameroon during the First World War, in which Spain was a neutral power. Independence came in 1968 as part of Equatorial Guinea, which also included the tiny island of Annobón, first sighted by European eyes on New Year's Day 1474. Although maps often show it for convenience next to Fernando Pó, Annobón actually lies about 350 miles away on the other side of São Tomé and Príncipe, at the other end of the chain of volcanic islands that continues the Cameroon Range out into the Atlantic.

A strange sort of country, you might think, stitching together the scraps of empire: a couple of islands and a little patch of continent, with the capital on an island rather than the mainland – the only country in the world apart from Denmark where this is the case. It is the smallest country in Africa by

[137] Including, appropriately enough, another Spanish possession off West Africa: La Gomera in the Canary Islands.

[138] In a further quirky coincidence (just the sort we like), the island is home to a monkey called the putty-nosed guenon, *Cercopithecus nictitans martini*, reportedly known as the 'cowardly monkey' because it is more often seen than heard, whose system of alarm calls is so sophisticated that it has been claimed they have a kind of language.

[139] Since then an even more profitable crop has been discovered: oil.

population, almost the smallest in area too, the smallest Spanish-speaking country in the world, and almost the only place in Africa where Spanish is an official language. In spite of the name, the equator does not actually run through Equatorial Guinea, but slightly to the south.[140]

The capital is Malabo, previously called Santa Isabel by the Spanish and Port Clarence by the British, and renamed in 1973 as part of a process of replacing European place names with African ones. Fernando Pó became Macías Nguema, a name that commemorated no less a personage than the President himself. The president in question was Macías Nguema Biyogo,[141] remembered as one of Africa's most bloody and klepto-maniacal tyrants. In 1979 he was finally overthrown and exe-cuted by his own nep-hew, Teodoro Obiang

Nguema Mbasogo, and the island formerly known as Formosa and Fernando Pó became Bioko.

Generally since then we have heard little enough of Equatorial Guinea, but then in 2004 came the startling news

[140] This is one Guinea that must be worth its weight in gold at pub quizzes.
[141] He Africanised his own name too, to Masie Nguema Biyogo Ñegue Ndong.

that Mark Thatcher, son of the former British prime minister, had been arrested in Cape Town and charged with supplying financial and logistical assistance to an alleged attempted coup organised by a South African mercenary called Simon Mann. Eventually he pleaded guilty to 'negligence' in buying an aircraft without taking sufficient care to find out about what it would be used for, and received a four-year suspended sentence and a fine of about half a million US dollars. He retained the inherited baronetcy awarded in 1991 to his father for being married to the prime minister.

Ebrauc

York seems a rather sedate place today, more reminiscent of teashops than blood-axes; but it was not ever thus. It was the Roman legionary fortress of *Eboracum*, and capital of the Roman province of *Britannia Inferior*; the Anglo-Saxons called it *Eoforwic*, and the Northmen who captured the city in 866 called it *Jórvik*. According to Nennius's *Historia Brittonum* the Celts called it *Caer* [Fortress] *Ebrauc*; and the modern Welsh form is *Efrog*.[142] All these names appear to come ultimately from the Brythonic *Ebórakon*, attested in the second century, which probably means the place of the yew trees.

The Latin name lives on in a few contexts in its abbreviated form as *Ebor*. The Archbishop of York signs himself Ebor: in place of his own surname, e.g. *David Ebor*. The Archbishop of York is the Primate of England, which sounds pretty grand until you realise that the Archbishop of Canterbury, *Cantuar*: is Primate of *All* England.

It also seems to have been called *Brigantium* (from the hill-fort still there, built by the Iron-age *Brigantes* who were there when the Romans arrived on the scene).[143] This is an era when hard facts are thin on the ground, but some historians think Ebrauc was more than just a name for the city of York – it was, they suggest, an entire independent Celtic kingdom which flourished, at least for a while, some time in the late fifth or early sixth century AD.

[142] The f is pronounced as a v.
[143] The name has also been applied to Betanzos in the province of La Coruña in northwest Spain, called after another tribe of the same name, and Bregenzon on the shores of Lake Constance in Austria, named after the *Brigantii*, a tribe possibly related to the *Brigantes*.

Then it was overrun by Deira, an Anglo-Saxon kingdom that controlled the territory between the Humber and the Tees, which at the end of the seventh century AD united with its northern neighbour Bernicia to form Northumbria. The Old English name Deira (*Deywr* in Brythonic) seems to be another reference to trees. Like Derry, it means the place of the oaks.

And now Northumbria, which once referred to a huge swathe of territory stretching all the way from Leeds to Edinburgh, has joined the list of obsolete place names – the modern county of Northumberland includes only a fraction of that area. However, there is a Northumbria University and a Northumbria Police, and the name is still used in a vaguer geographical and historical sense to refer to the northeast of England, as the obsolete Strathclyde is in the West of Scotland.

The same applies to Wessex, another of the major Anglo-Saxon kingdoms which has not had any official use since the eleventh century but which has continued in occasional poetic use, especially since Thomas Hardy popularised it as the name of the setting of his West Country novels. In 1999, in honour of his marriage to Sophie Rhys-Jones, Prince Edward received the title of Earl of Wessex, a style that had not been used for more than 900 years. The last incumbent was called Harold Godwinson. If you remember, he came to a sticky end, in the course of a certain battle on the coast of Sussex that took place in 1066. Most people think it was an arrow in the eye that did for him, but you can't believe everything you read in the tapestries.

Republic of Rose Island

So there you are, you're only human, you want to have your own country and be its absolute monarch – after all, who doesn't? But where to find one? You could just launch an invasion and steal someone else's place, and that has certainly been a popular method over the centuries. However, there's no getting away from it, that kind of behaviour is bound to cause ill feeling and store up problems for future generations.

You could exploit a constitutional grey area over some forgotten little feudal state, as the flower-grower Giorgio Carbone, his 'Tremendousness'[144] the self-styled Prince Giorgio of Seborga, did in the 1960s when he claimed that this ancient principality, which had been sold to Sardinia in 1729 but inexplicably overlooked by the Congress of Vienna in 1815 and the Act of Unification of the Kingdom of Italy in 1861, was therefore not part of the modern Italian state.

You could adopt the direct approach and, promising faithfully not to rebel against her imperial authority, just ask the Queen to give you a little uninhabited bit of her empire that no one seems to care about, as Matthew Dowdy Shiell, father of the slightly famous novelist M P (Matthew Phipps) Shiel,[145] did in 1865 when he founded the Kingdom of Redonda, on an island that soulless literalists take to be part of Antigua and Barbuda. Incredibly, it worked.

You could do as bookseller Richard Booth did one April

[144] *sua Tremendità*
[145] Sic. Seemingly his idea of rebelling against parental authority was to drop one letter from his surname.

Fool's Day in the 1970s, and descend on an unsuspecting little town in the Welsh Marches, bearing a sceptre made out of a sink plunger; then simply declare yourself King of Hay-on-Wye and start flogging peerages.[146]

You could seize some rusting hulk of a wartime anti-aircraft installation out in the North Sea just outside British territorial waters, call it Sealand, install millions of pounds worth of computer hardware and high-speed satellite links, start offering no-questions-asked secure hosting facilities to the world, and see if anyone really cares enough to try and stop you.

You could adopt the wimp's approach and do the whole thing on the Internet; or, for the truly entry-level nation-builder, declare sovereignty over your own flat and make a TV programme about it, as comedian Danny Wallace did.[147] Snug in your fantasy virtual republic, or curled up on the royal sofa/throne, you should be safe enough from the palace coup, the assassin's bomb and the revolutionary firing squad.

Because, if dealing with real territory, you do have to bear in mind the risk that some powerful neighbouring state, for example one that actually has a real live army of some kind, will take your little project too seriously and put a stop it. Even if you are not occupying anything worth having, somewhere with no mineral resources or strategic value, and are causing no trouble to anyone, your idealistic intentions and/or lovable chutzpah may be seen as a territorial challenge and, unless you have very powerful friends, your

---

[146] That seems to have worked well enough as well: thirty years later, his annual literary festival brings in some 70,000 visitors and injects a welcome £3,000,000 or so into the local economy, not to mention big-league acts such as Bill Clinton, who describes the place as 'a Woodstock of the mind' and 'my kinda town'.

[147] Which brings to mind an old joke: Prince Rainier of Monaco is visiting the United States, and President Bush takes him to see the Astrodome in Houston, Texas, with its 710-foot dome covering 9½ acres. 'Don't you wish you had something like this in your country?' he asks proudly. 'Ah, Mr President,' replies his Serene Highness, 'then we would have the world's only indoor country.'

neutrality is not likely to be guaranteed by anyone.[148]

1968 was a year of turmoil. The streets of Paris seemed to be witnessing another revolution. The Vietnam War raged on, and Russian tanks rolled into Prague to cancel the Spring. Martin Luther King was assassinated, at the height of the American Civil Rights movement, while in Britain Enoch Powell raved about rivers of blood. But it was also a time of liberation and independence for many nations, with the process of decolonisation started in the 1950s continuing apace[149] and human-kind setting its sights on the moon itself. If ever there was a time to start a new nation, this was surely it.

In Italy an engineer called Giorgio Rosa[150] had been building himself an artificial island in the form of a steel platform in the Adriatic seven miles off Rimini, and in June 1968 he declared independence from Italy as the Republic of Rose Island. Or rather, *la Respubliko de la Insulo de la Rozoj*, since the official language of the place was to be (of course) Esperanto. Clearly just as good with money as with steel pylons, Engineer Rosa installed facilities worthy of a small town: not just a souvenir

---

[148] Who would have thought that, only fifty years ago, the United Kingdom would formally declare sovereignty over Rockall, a desolate lump of rock 287 miles from the Scottish mainland, and bother to occupy it? Was it just national machismo, or something to do with controlling Soviet maritime spying?

[149] Pleasant Island and Portuguese Guinea to name but two examples.

[150] George Rose, if you like.

shop, bar and restaurant but a nightclub and a post office too. He devised a very pretty orange flag with three roses on a white escutcheon, and issued stamps. Even though many people own houses larger than his republic (surface area about a tenth of an acre), the economic prospects as a novelty tourist destination, tax-free of course, seemed rather promising. Perhaps that was its downfall. Of course, there could have been other very lucrative reasons for being outside the reach of Italian law: did the facilities include a casino? A brothel? The rumours flew.

Whatever the reason, the Italian authorities were not long in reacting. Carabinieri and tax inspectors boarded the platform and took it over. The Rose Island government in exile sent a telegram of protest to Italy, but it was the only state to do so. No diplomatic official was carpeted, not a single ambassador recalled; the governments of the free world stood by in the face of this unprovoked aggression and did nothing. The novelty stamps were still available, now overprinted with the words 'under Italian military occupation'.

Talk about breaking a butterfly upon a wheel. The platform was summarily dynamited, and though its creator reportedly gained some satisfaction from seeing just how much dynamiting it took to demolish his sturdy structure, it was not Heligoland. What little remained of the Rose Republic was washed away in a storm not long after.

Ever defiant, President Giorgio issued commemorative stamps depicting the explosion. Along the bottom, in Latin this time, were the proud, poignant words *HOSTIUM RABIES DIRUIT OPUS NON IDEAM*. The fury of the enemy may destroy the edifice – but not the idea.

Madras

Bombay to Mumbai we can understand, likewise Calcutta to Kolkata and Benares to Varanasi – a slight phonetic adjustment towards the local form no doubt – but how did Madras become the unrecognisable Chennai in 1996?

As we have seen, place names are highly political things, and attempting to put back the clock to a time before injustice can be fraught with complications. With Pondicherry (French *Pondichéry*, changed back to Tamil *Puducherry*, 'new village', in 2006) the case seems straight-forward enough, as does the replacement of Calcutta with Kolkata in 2000 to reflect Bengali pronunciation. But how far back should we go? The name of Calcutta/Kolkata probably comes from one of the three villages on the site of which the city was built: Kalikata, which in turn comes from *Kalikshetra*, 'Land of the goddess Kali', so perhaps that should be the name. Then again, it might be from Bengali *kilkila* meaning a flat area, or from *kali* ('lime') and *kata* ('burned shell') after the industry of making shell-lime, or from its location on the bank of a canal (*khal*).

But there are many names for Calcutta. The British East India Company arrived in 1690 and made the place their Bengal headquarters; later it was capital of the entire Raj from 1772 to 1911. Thanks to its new civic architecture it became known as the City of Palaces, while the less salubrious 'native' quarter was nicknamed Black Town. Kipling, borrowing a phrase coined by the Scottish poet James 'Bysshe Vanolis' Thomson in 1880 for his nightmarish vision of London, called it the City of Dreadful Night. On the other hand, and the other bank of the River Hooghly, in

Dominique Lapierre's 1985 novel, lay the 'City of Joy',[151] Anandnagar.

The British immediately set to work fortifying their base against attack; it was named Fort William after William III.[152] Completed in 1706, it was taken fifty years later by the Nawab of Bengal, who renamed the place Alinagar, and this was the location of the infamous Black Hole of Calcutta, the 18-by-14-foot guardroom where, according to a contemporary account, all but 23 of 146[153] British prisoners died of suffocation and heat exhaustion.

But why go changing names fifty years after independence, when surely India must have long since completed the process of symbolically re-asserting ownership of its national institutions? The *Times* newspaper's verdict at the time of the Madras/Chennai rebranding was that 'name-changing is an Indian obsession', which can even be 'a sycophantic gesture to a powerful politician or family'.

[151] Now the name of a children's charity working with slum children in Calcutta and West Bengal.
[152] As were the Fort William built before the American Civil War in Boston harbour in 1643, and the Fort William and Mary in 1632 at Portsmouth, New Hampshire. Fort William was also at one time the name of the 1625 fortification, variously known as Fort Amsterdam, Fort James, Fort Anne, Fort George and Fort Willem Hendrick, at New Amsterdam, later New Orange or, as we know it today, New York.
[153] Research suggests the real figure was probably about 60.

So it's not just a matter of replacing a historically mangled European version of a name with its 'correct' Indian form: issues of language and religion soon raise their ugly heads. India speaks many tongues; most are related to each other, being members of the Indo-European family that includes nearly all the languages of Europe. But about one in four of the Indian population, some 200 million people, speak a language from the unrelated Dravidian group, such as Kannada, Malayalam or Tamil.

Often what lies behind a name-change is not just an increasing desire for regional identity but a power shift from Muslim to Hindu, as in the case of campaigns championed by the Hindu nationalist party Shiv Sena, who would 'right the wrongs' of Mughal names for Hindu places, such as Allahabad, in Sanskrit *Prayag*. In a country that has been, in the words of Saeed Jaffrey's character in the film *My Beautiful Laundrette*, 'sodomised by religion', controversy seems inevitable. Some claim that an English name, besides reflecting the history of a place, is actually more neutral and acceptable to all sections of the community.

There is certainly no shortage of opposition among Indian commentators. According to the author and diplomat Shashi Tharoor, the change to Chennai is based on linguistic ignorance. Mr M [Muthuvel] Karunanidhi, chief minister of what Tharoor calls the 'chauvinist' government of Tamil Nadu,[154] was simply wrong in claiming that Madras was not a Tamil name. 'Bad history is worse lexicology,' declares Tharoor, 'but in India it is good politics.'

The British East India Company arrived in what became Madras in 1639 and began to fortify it on 23 April 1640; they called it Fort St George. The subsequent conurbation took in a place called Madraspatnam, i.e. Madras (*patnam* meaning town), also known as Chennapatnam or Chinnepatan. Madras was perceived as being of Portuguese origin, perhaps from a trader called Madeiros or a fisherman called Madarasan or a

[154] Formerly Madras State.

prince called Madrie, but in fact it may be from the Sanskrit *Mandarstra*, 'Kingdom of Manda', or even the Tamil for honey, *madhu-ras*. Chennai, meanwhile, is said by respectable authorities not to be of Tamil origin at all, but from Chennappa Naicker, the Raja of Chandragiri, a Telugu speaker from Andhra Pradesh, who granted the British trading rights along the coast. Which is the 'colonial' name now?

A measure of how careful you have to be with theories of name origins is given by the tall story told about the name Bangalore, soon to be rebranded under its Kannada name, Bengaluru. The king, Vira Ballala, lost his way while out hunting. When an old woman offered him some boiled beans he was so grateful that he named the place after the dish: Benda Kalaru, city of beans. Such primitive associations are a thing of the past, now that Bangalore is a hub of India's high-tech economy; today it is the city of call centres, and in America to be 'Bangalored' is to lose your job when the work is outsourced to a cheaper labour market.

The name-changing 'obsession' continues. As well as Bangalore to Bengaluru, keep an eye out for such makeovers as West Bengal to Bangla, Patna to Pataliputra and Lucknow to Lakshmanpuri. Even Delhi may change its name, though whether to Dilli,[155] Hastinapur or Indraprastha remains to be seen. Leaving aside all the tabloid quips about Mumbai mix and Mollywood, should we start referring to India as Bharat?

---

[155] This would be confusing given that the capital of East Timor is also called Dilli.

Königsberg

Since the demise of the Soviet Union in 1991, this little chunk of Russia outside Russia, separated from the motherland by the Baltic states of Estonia, Latvia and Lithuania, has stood out more sorely and thumblike than ever. But its early influences were from the west, not the east.

Königsberg ('king's mountain') was named after the Bohemian king Premysl Otakar II, who had a fortress built there in 1255 by the Teutonic Knights on the site of an ancient settlement called Tvanksta[156]. Its fortunes ebbed and flowed through the subsequent centuries like the inconveniently shifting silt in the channels of its harbour. Having been destroyed in 1263 by the Prussians, in 1340 the rebuilt city became part of the Hanseatic League, the alliance that monopolised Baltic trade for four hundred years, and from 1525 until 1618 it was the residence of the dukes of Prussia. In 1701 Elector Frederick III of Brandenburg crowned himself Frederick I of Prussia there.

Mathematicians may have heard of Königsberg because of something called the Seven Bridges Problem. The question, formulated in 1736 by the Swiss mathematician Leonhard Euler, is whether it is possible to trace a route around the city and over the River Pregel using each bridge once and once only. The answer (look away now if you want to work it out for yourself) is no. Euler proved that such a route, a 'Eulerian path', is possible only if there are at most two nodes of odd degree, as they came to be called in the new discipline of graph theory.

---

[156] Also spelled, at the risk of sounding like a verb declension, Twangste, Tvangeste, Twoyngst, Twongst.

The name Königsberg has a small but distinctive place in the history of the First World War. A ship of that name was stationed in, as it happens, a place called Tanganyika, and put into the Rufiji Delta for repairs. There she was cornered by British cruisers and crippled by their guns. The captain scuttled the ship and joined the land army of General Paul von Lettow-Vorbeck, who went on to hold German East Africa against vastly superior Allied forces until the end of the war. These few thousand men, mostly sailors, reservists and native Askaris, were cut off and outnumbered ten to one but held out until two days after Armistice Day, when news reached them of the defeat of Germany.

In the twentieth century, however, the winds of change started to blow from the east. The Russians, having unsuccessfully besieged the city in the First World War, spent two months reducing it to rubble at the end of the Second.[157] The entire German population was expelled in 1947, and long lines of bedraggled refugees marched to Germany. Königsberg passed into the Soviet Union as Kaliningrad, named after Mikhail Ivanovich Kalinin,[158] and became a major industrial and commercial centre, closed to foreigners – a contrast with its elegant historical past as a city of government and education, the birthplace of the 'sage of Königsberg' Immanuel Kant. On the ruins of the thirteenth-century Königsberg Castle they built a brutally ugly concrete structure called the *Dom Sovetov* or House of the Soviets, never finished and itself now a ruin, apparently sinking into the collapsed foundations of the castle.

Sad to say, the place is not what it was. But it still has one valuable resource. Kaliningrad, or more precisely the 'blue earth'[159] of the peninsula of Sambia (*Samland*), has rich deposits of succinum nodules – better known as amber. Long

[157] British air raids had taken their toll as well.
[158] The Chairman of the Presidium of the Supreme Soviet in whose honour Tver became Kalinin from 1931 to 1990.
[159] Marine glauconitic sands in the Lower Oligocene strata, to you geologists.

prized as a semiprecious 'stone',[160] amber has long been prized – and faked – for such fancy goods as rosary beads, chessmen, jewellery, cigarette holders, and of course the mouthpieces of those old-fashioned pipes of the type Sherlock Holmes is often pictured using. The Greek word for amber is *elektron*, and this is where we get our word 'electricity', a reference to the way amber easily becomes statically charged so that it picks up light objects. The word 'amber' originally referred to what we now call ambergris (literally 'grey amber'), the strange waxy substance seen floating in tropical seas, which is actually a secretion from the bile duct of the sperm whale.[161]

The German for amber is Bernstein, 'burn-stone', which apart from being a common Jewish surname,[162] reflects the fact that it will actually catch light if heated sufficiently. Which leads us to one of the great mysteries of the Second World War, something called the *Bernsteinzimmer* or Amber Room. In the Catherine Palace, the summer residence of the Russian tsars at Tsarskoe Selo near Saint Petersburg, there was a room entirely panelled and decorated in amber, gold leaf and mirrors. Created at the beginning of the eighteenth century and gifted to Peter the Great by Frederick William I, the 'Soldier King' of Prussia, in order to cement their alliance against the Swedes, it was looted by the Nazis during the war

[160] Really amber is just fossil resin that has reached a stable state through the loss of its more volatile constituents: no mineralisation is involved.

[161] This sweetly pungent substance was used as a spice in perfumery and even in cooking; Alexander Pope wrote that 'Praise is like ambergris; a little whiff of it, by snatches, is very agreeable; but when a man holds a whole lump of it to his nose, it is a stink and strikes you down.' Much puzzlement existed over what the stuff actually was and where it came from. A sixteenth-century natural history gives us a hint of how the word amber came to refer to the resin: 'Great variety of Opinions hath there been concerning Amber. Some think it to be a Gum that distils from Trees: Others tell us, it is made of Whales Dung; or else of their Sperm or Seed'. During the Renaissance it was worn as jewellery, which presumably is what links the meanings of 'grey' and 'yellow' amber.

[162] At this point we might also namecheck Woody Allen, born Allen Stewart Konigsberg.

and taken to Königsberg to be displayed in the castle.

Its fate after that is unknown, though there is no shortage of theories. Was it hidden in mine workings or in Lake Toplitz in the Austrian Alps where Nazi gold and counterfeit sterling notes and who knows what else are rumoured to have been stashed? Did it go to a watery grave on board a torpedoed submarine? Do the amber panels, all 6 tons and 600 square feet of them, still lie under the ruins of Königsberg Castle, blown up by the Russians in the 1960s in order to destroy the vestiges of Prussian militarism? Or was it simply destroyed *in situ* when the castle was burned out at the end of the war?

A painstaking eight-million-dollar reconstruction of the Amber Room was installed in the Catherine Palace in 2003. The task of economic and cultural reconstruction in Königsberg/Kaliningrad, with its crumbling buildings and rusting naval dockyards, will surely be an even more arduous one.

Chagos Islands

About 300 miles south of the Maldives, 1,000 miles southwest of India and 1,200 miles northeast of Mauritius, lies a tiny speckle of islands called the Chagos. The largest of them, a tiny spermatozoid squiggle lost in the vastness of the Indian Ocean, is called Diego Garcia. But if your atlas is up to date it will probably use the official designation invented in 1965: British Indian Ocean Territory, or BIOT.

Normally in such remote spots you are left pretty much alone, but just occasionally the outside world finds out you have something it wants – mineral deposits, tourist potential – and beats a path to your door.[163] Sometimes that very geographical remoteness can be the desirable commodity. Rather than just commanding a few rivermouths, as Heligoland did, strategic importance for today's military can be about providing a vital foothold in the middle of the ocean, where ships can refuel, planes can take off, global communications can be monitored and, dare we say, political detainees can be quietly taken for some extra-special questioning away from the prying eyes of the international community and the restrictive laws of the home territory. And Diego Garcia is not just any old chunk of coral, but a perfect natural harbour inside which there is room, so it's said, to berth the entire US Navy.[164] Such a place is worth its weight in any commodity you care to mention, and its inhabitants should be able to name their price.

Unless, of course, they happen to be so few and friendless that no purchase is necessary.

[163] The results can be disastrous for the locals, as in the case of Nauru and St Kilda.
[164] Heaven spare us from the nightmarish end-time scenario in which such a need might ever arise.

It's not clear where the name Diego Garcia comes from, but the islands were discovered by the Portuguese in the early sixteenth century. They became a dependency of Mauritius, first under French and then British rule. The Chagos were a profitable source of coconut oil, which apparently fuelled the streetlamps of London at one time, and copra, the dried meat of the coconut. Some 400 million nuts a year were harvested by people known as Chagossians or *Îlois* ('islanders'), whose ancestors had been imported by the French as slaves in the eighteenth century, and later as indentured workers from Africa and India. They speak a French-based Indian Ocean creole that would mystify a Parisian.

Then came the Cold War, and the conviction that only American military might could save the world from perdition. Diego Garcia was just the spot for keeping tabs on Soviet activity in the Indian Ocean, especially when an alliance with India seemed likely. The place belonged to the British, always so helpful in handing over odd bits of territory and not interfering in the way they were run. And the US would start with a clean slate: they wanted the place 'swept' of its inhabitants, 'sanitised', leaving nothing but seagulls. What to do with the humans? Sir Denis Greenhill, then head of the diplomatic service, supplied the answer in a memo to Britain's UN ambassador: 'Unfortunately, along with the seagulls go some few Tarzans and Man Fridays . . . who are hopefully being wished on to Mauritius.'

So the Tarzans and Man Fridays were encouraged in various ways to leave. Those who were away on Mauritius found themselves barred from returning. In what seemed like a kind of grim warning, pet dogs were rounded up and gassed. Eventually the remaining population was shipped out to Mauritius and simply dumped in the slums of Port Louis. Not surprisingly many have since died through illness, suicide or despair.

Surely there must be laws against that kind of thing? Yes. Article 73 of the UN Human Rights Charter obliges nations responsible for 'territories whose peoples have not yet attained a full measure of self-government' to 'recognise the principle that the interests of the inhabitants of these territories are paramount, and accept as a sacred trust the obligation to promote to the utmost . . . the wellbeing of the inhabitants of these territories', including 'their just treatment, and their protection against abuses'.

Instead, the very existence of a native population was denied; in order to 'give us a defensible position to take up at the UN', the government planned[165] to 'maintain the fiction that the inhabitants of the Chagos are not a permanent or semi-permanent population. The Ordinance would be published in the *BIOT Gazette*, which has only very limited circulation. Publicity will therefore be minimal.' When the story started to emerge, Her Majesty's Government responded with cynical and barefaced lies. 'There is nothing in our files about a population and an evacuation,' they said. Five years later this had changed to 'all went willingly and none were coerced'. The islands had been 'uninhabited': the only people there were migrant workers who were perfectly happy to leave.

[165] 'More or less fraudulently' as one official uneasily noted.

According to a report in the *Guardian*, Britain's reward from the Americans was an $11.5 million discount on Polaris nuclear submarines. What did the exiled Chagossians get? In 1973 the princely sum of £650,000 was awarded in 'full and final discharge of HMG's obligations' via the government of Mauritius.[166] In March 1982 a slightly less trivial amount was forthcoming – £4 million, but still cheap at the price as a way of tricking the islanders into signing away all claim on their homeland by means of a thumbprint on a legal document in a foreign language.

Forty years on, the Chagossians – British citizens – are still living on Mauritius, some in abject poverty. In 2001 a High Court ruling granted them the right to return, but that decision was simply overturned, more or less with a stroke of the pen, by something called an order in council. The Secretary of State simply decrees, without reference to Parliament, that it must be so; the monarch signs the order, and the ancient royal prerogative trumps any democratic or accountable institution. Thus, under the British Indian Ocean Territory (Immigration) Order 2004, any unauthorised presence became punishable by a three-year prison sentence.

In May 2006 the High Court hit back and declared the ruling illegal, pointing out that it was not concerned with the interests of the territory itself but those of the United Kingdom and the United States. The judges expressed themselves in strong terms: 'The suggestion that a minister can, through the means of an order in council, exile a whole population from a British overseas territory and claim that he is doing so for the "peace, order and good government" of the territory is, to us, repugnant. The defendant's approach to this case involves much clanking of the "chains of the ghosts of the past".'

The Chagossians' campaign continues, and has many friends. David Snoxell, British High Commissioner to Mauritius from 2000 to 2004, put the point forcefully in February 2007: 'Is it not time that HMG brought together Chagossian leaders,

---

[166] It took five years to reach them.

Mauritius and the US to sort out this relic of the Cold War and rectify one of the worst violations of fundamental human rights perpetrated by the UK in the twentieth century?'

Back at 'DG', B-52 bombers, tankers, AWACS surveillance planes and anti-submarine aircraft operate from a 12,000-foot runway, flying missions to such places as Iraq, Afghanistan and Somalia. A naval refuelling and support station assures command of the Indian Ocean; the USAF Space Command runs a satellite tracking station and communications facility, and NASA has an emergency landing site for the space shuttle. The original fifty-year lease runs out in 2016 but can easily be renewed. The UK has supposedly promised to return the islands to Mauritius when they are no longer needed for defence purposes, but it's hard to see when that might be.

Will the islanders ever return? The British government has spilled plenty of ink arguing it could never be. The islands are no longer inhabitable by civilians; not only are there rising sea levels (from which the military are somehow immune), but security would be compromised, even though, as the Commonwealth Secretary-General has pointed out, the outlying islands are in some cases hundred of miles from the base. As *The Times* observed back in 1983, 'the contrast with the treatment of the Falklanders could not be more stark. All British citizens are equal but some, it seems, are more equal than others.'

Cathures

It is safe to say that no one reading this remembers a time when the name Cathures was in current use, since it has been obsolete for about a thousand years.[167] In fact, no one is absolutely certain where that name came from or what exactly it referred to, but it was probably a beautiful spot by the banks of a shallow salmon river, the site of one of Britain's earliest Christian foundations. The Romans are said to have had a trading post there by around AD 80. The Celtic saint Ninian went there in the year 380 and consecrated a burial ground, but nothing much else happened until St Kentigern[168] arrived in the sixth century. He and his monks liked the place so much they stayed and built a fine cathedral, which miraculously survived the Reformation. Daniel Defoe visited the place in 1723 and declared it 'the cleanest and beautifullest and best built City in Britain, London excepted'. By that time it was known by a different Celtic name,[169] the meaning of which is debated but often said to be 'the Dear Green Place'. Today we know it as the city of Glasgow.

[167] *Cathures* is the title of a collection of poems by Edwin Morgan, and the name of a local chamber choir, but otherwise the word is all but forgotten today.

[168] More often referred to by the diminutive form Mungo.

[169] *Glaschu.*

Yugoslavia

The Balkans are almost proverbial for historical and ethnic complexity. To unravel this patchwork of statelets, principalities and corners of empire – or perhaps kaleidoscope would be a better image – would take more space and more insight than this little volume can offer. For those of us whose view of Europe was formed in the second half of the twentieth century, therefore, it was perhaps a blessing that everything from Slavonia to Banat to the Free State of Fiume and the Sanjak of Novibazar could be lumped together as 'Yugoslavia'. A convenient fiction, certainly, a ragbag of uncategorisable odds and ends – we had some idea what a Greek or a Turk was, but who knew what a 'Yugoslav' looked like or what it ate for breakfast? – but at least people would understand when you told them where you'd been on holiday.

At the end of the First World War a 'Kingdom of the Serbs, Croats and Slovenes' was formed from the Slavic provinces of the defunct empire of Austria-Hungary (Slovenia, Croatia, Bosnia and Herzegovina), together with Serbia and Montenegro, and Macedonian territory ceded from Bulgaria. The ensuing Kingdom of Yugoslavia,[170] the 'First Yugoslavia', was reborn in 1943 after a two-year wartime hiatus as the 'Second Yugoslavia', which went by various names including Democratic Federal Yugoslavia or the Democratic Federation of Yugoslavia, the Federal People's Republic of Yugoslavia and the Socialist Federal Republic of Yugoslavia, which finally became the Federal Republic of Yugoslavia. It consisted (until 1992) of Serbia[171] (book-ended by its two semi-autonomous

[170] A word meaning simply the country of the Southern Slavs.
[171] Previously spelled 'Servia'.

provinces of Vojvodina and Kosovo), Croatia, Bosnia-Herzegovina, Slovenia, Montenegro[172] and Macedonia.

Then came the nightmarish cataclysm of the 1990s, and everything shattered back into myriad states too small even to be labelled clearly on a normal-sized map of Europe. Suddenly the word Yugoslavia was always preceded by the word

'former', meaning presumably 'the area we used to call Yugoslavia before pieces started being lopped off it', but perhaps giving a misleading impression that there was no longer a country of that name (like 'the former Soviet Union'). In fact, there was still a Yugoslavia until 2003, long after it had fallen out of the headlines – albeit a much smaller one consisting only of Serbia and Montenegro. The name Yugoslavia was dropped in favour of, logically enough, 'Serbia and Montenegro', and in 2006 the two states went their own separate ways as, naturally, 'Serbia' and 'Montenegro'.

And today there are people of voting age whose world has never included a Yugoslavia, and who indeed may never even have heard of such a place.

---

[172] The Italian name of Crna Gora ('black mountain').

Gilbert and Ellice Islands

In the bad old days of British colonialism, it wasn't necessary to be all that famous to have an island named after you. You certainly didn't need to be a seafarer of any kind. When Captain Arent de Peyster, the American commander of the British brigantine *Rebecca*, stumbled on[173] the atoll of Funafuti, he simply named the islands after the owner of his cargo: Edward Ellice (1783–1863), a London merchant and financier and Member of Parliament for Coventry. The Lord Chancellor, Henry Brougham, described Ellice as 'large and rich and stupid' – and, well, he was certainly a big man and not short of a penny or two. The Gilbert Islands were named after another Englishman, Captain Thomas Gilbert, but this time by an Estonian admiral in the Russian navy, Adam Johann von Krusenstern.

A British protectorate since 1892 and a Crown Colony since 1916, the Gilbert and Ellice Islands were a rather ill-matched pair. The smaller Ellice Islands broke away in 1975 and became Tuvalu, which turned out to be an economic windfall in the Internet age: Tuvalu's 'top-level domain name' (TLD), the bit at the end of the URL or Internet address, is '.tv' and that is worth money to corporations who want to have an online presence that shouts TELEVISION!

The Gilbert Islands became independent in 1979 as Kiribati. This might seem just as different from the colonial name as Tuvalu is from Ellice, but in fact it is no more or less than the local pronunciation and spelling of 'Gilberts', the combination 'ti' being pronounced 's' in Gilbertese (a.k.a. Kiribati,

---

[173] It seems the right word, if it's true that land was sighted only three ship-lengths away.

Kiribatese or *taetae ni Kiribati*, the language of Kiribati, which has had a written form since the 1840s).[174]

Of the 33 islands that make up the Republic of Kiribati (*Ribaberikin Kiribati*), only 20 are inhabited. The population is concentrated in the sixteen Gilbert Islands, which straddle the Equator. The largest is Kiritimati, formerly known as (can you guess?) Christmas Island, 'discovered' by Captain James Cook on 24 December 1777. It should not be confused with another Christmas Island in the Indian Ocean, sighted in 1615 by Richard Rowe of the *Thomas*, named on Christmas Day 1643 by Captain William Mynors of the British East India Company and administered by Australia since 1958.

No, this is the famous Christmas Island of the nuclear-weapon tests of the late 1950s, the so-called Operation Grapple. The H-bombs were exploded in the air rather than on the ground, leaving a strange uprooted mushroom cloud floating in the blue sky. The intensity of the flash at the moment of detonation is hard to imagine. The servicemen were given blindfolds and ordered to face away from the explosion with their hands over their eyes. Even so, as one

---

[174] One is reminded of George Bernard Shaw's facetious re-spelling of the English word 'fish' as 'ghoti': gh as in laugh, o as in women and ti as in nation.

witness wrote, 'at that instant I was able to see straight through my hands. I could see the veins. I could see the blood, I could see all the skin tissue, I could see the bones and worst of all, I could see the flash itself. It was like looking into a white-hot diamond, a second sun.' The result of the tests, for better or worse, was Britain's ability to make a one-megaton nuclear bomb less than a ton in weight, and its entry into the (then) exclusive club of thermonuclear powers. The effects on the servicemen present, not to mention the temporarily evacuated islanders, are a matter of long-running controversy.

With the Gilbertese phosphate deposits exhausted, and given that the TLD '.ki' doesn't do anything particularly special for your website, the economy is based on coconut products and fishing rights. And of course the islands have the usual problems of lack of arable land and the presence of a relentlessly encroaching globally warmed ocean. We can only wish them a very merry *Kiritimati*, and hope they may see many more.

Canadaway

The Americans, you may have noticed, are not like us.

For example, they make quite different use of words like 'city' and 'town' and 'village'. You may imagine there are no villages in the USA, only 'small towns'. Not so. In some parts of America, such as New York State, a village is a settlement of any size – perhaps home to ten or twenty thousand souls – while a town is an administrative area second only to a county. Thus it is that the city of Batavia (population 16,256 in 2000) is in – though not part of – the town of Batavia (pop. 5,915, area about 50 square miles) in Genesee County (pop. 60,370), New York State (pop. 18,976,457).

Likewise, about 50 miles away on the southern shores of Lake Eyrie, just south of the city of Dunkirk (pop. 13,131), which is surrounded by the town of Dunkirk (pop. 1,387), in Chautauqua County (pop. 139,750), we find the town of Pomfret (pop. 14,703) within which lies a village called Fredonia (pop. 10,706). It was settled at the turn of the nineteenth century in a place previously known as Canadaway, from a Native American word *Ganadawao* meaning a place among hemlocks.

You may be thinking that there is a letter missing in this discussion – surely Freedonia? Yes indeed, if you have in mind the 1933 Marx brothers film *Duck Soup*, the action of which classic satire takes place in the fictional European country of Freedonia, 'the Land of the Spree and the Home of the Knave'.[175]

---

[175] The name has often been adopted as a convenient joke name for any obscure far-off country, as well as – of course – a short-lived online micronation.

The name Fredonia was likewise coined, though some 130 years earlier, on the basis of the English word 'freedom'. It was even proposed (by the politician Samuel Latham Mitchill) as a replacement for the allegedly prosaic and uninspiring term 'United States of America'. Because of this there are a surprising number of Fredonias in the USA – Arizona, Arkansas, Iowa, Kansas, Kentucky, Michigan, North Dakota, Pennsylvania, Texas and Wisconsin all run to one – but the New York Fredonia has a particular claim to fame. The story goes that when *Duck Soup* came out the mayor of Fredonia, one Harry B Hickey, wrote a pompous letter of complaint in the following terms: 'The name of Fredonia has been without a blot since 1817. I feel it is my duty as Mayor to question your intentions in using the name of our city in your picture.'

'Your Excellency,' came the reply, 'Our advice is that you change the name of your town. It is hurting our picture.'

Free City of Danzig

Where and what is, or was, Danzig? Is it Poland or Germany? Much blood has been shed over that question.

Today it's very much in Poland and we call it by the Polish name, Gdansk, or if you're a stickler for accents, Gdańsk.[176] Before the Second World War it was known in English as Danzig, sometimes variously spelled Dantzig, Dantzic or Dantsic. To many of the locals it is Gdańsk, since this is the capital of the region of Kashubia, which has its own language. Kashubian (or Cassubian) is a dialect of Pomeranian related to Slovincian; like Polish, it's a West Slavic language, but a distinct language. Another name for the area is Pomerelia; it's the eastern part of Pomerania, which also includes something called Pomesania.[177]

This area, historically ruled by the Prussians, has always been an important trading port, Poland's only outlet to the Baltic. But it is very much a place of its own, a member of the Hanseatic League since 1361 and a bustling multi-ethnic city with significant Russian, Jewish, Dutch and even Scottish communities. It is the fate of such places to be fought over by neighbouring powers like dogs scrapping for a bone, and this one played a not insignificant part in the start of two world wars. But at two brief moments in history it has stood proudly alone as the Free City of Danzig.

In 1793 Danzig became part of the Kingdom of Prussia, then

---

[176] The acute accent on the n denotes a 'palatal' sound like the one in Spanish *mañana*.

[177] Going west from Gdańsk (or Eastern) Pomerania we find the regions of Farther Pomerania and Hither Pomerania, which last would make a splendid war cry, or perhaps the title of a nineteenth-century historical romance. There was also a Pogesania, but let's not worry about that now.

the German Empire in 1871, until 1919. Thus, though the surrounding territory is undeniably Polish (or more accurately Kashubian), the population of Danzig was overwhelmingly German. In 1807, during the Napoleonic Wars, the city was taken by the French and declared a 'Free City', also known as the Republic of Danzig. However, this was something of a misnomer since in practice it meant tens of thousands of French troops being billeted on the hapless burghers and the city being taxed till the pips squeaked. With the port blockaded by the British, the city had to print money in the form of *assignats*, a kind of government bond used during the French Revolution. Hyperinflation, and then disease and starvation, set in; the French abandoned the city to the Russians and Prussians in 1814 and the Congress of Vienna formalised its reincorporation into Prussia the following year.

The Free City of Danzig that you are more likely to have heard of was created by the Treaty of Versailles after the First World War. It was Polish territory for purposes of customs and

foreign policy, administered by a *Deutscher Volksrat* (German Council) modelled on the Weimar constitution, but under League of Nations sovereignty. A 'Polish Corridor' connected it to Germany. It was not a happy compromise; Poland felt its all-important seaport compromised, a sensitive subject for a nation so long deprived of any coastline, and the city's German majority felt straightforwardly German. By the eve of the Second World War ethnic Germans constituted 95 per cent of the population, and these Germans saw themselves as part of the greater Germany that Hitler was moving towards assembling by whatever means necessary. On 1 September 1939 the German battleship *Schleswig-Holstein*[178] opened fire on the Polish garrison and Danzig was formally annexed by Nazi Germany. In the process of retaking the city, Allied and Soviet bombardment, followed by the looting and pillaging of the Red Army, reduced it to ruins. Like Dresden, Ypres, Hiroshima or Heligoland, it had to be rebuilt from the ground up. Among the many twin cities of Gdańsk is, appropriately enough, Kaliningrad, its Russian cousin on the other side of the Gulf of Gdansk.

One of Danzig's most famous sons is the German novelist Günther Grass.[179] In *The Tin Drum*, the first part of his Danzig Trilogy, he describes how a city built over seven centuries burned down in three days. Bells melted quietly down the walls of their belfries. The Fleischergaße (Butchers' Street) burned with the smell of Sunday roast; in the Milchkannengaße (Milk Churn Street) the milk boiled in the churns; and in the Kleinen Hossenähergaße (Little Hosemakers' Street) the fire was measured for many pairs of flame-red trousers. It was hardly the first time Danzig had been put to the torch, having been at one time or another sacked by Pomeranians, Brandenburgers, Teutonic Knights, Poles, Swedes, Frenchmen, Prussians and Russians, almost as if a regular pruning by fire every generation or so were necessary to ensure the continuing vigour of a city.

The German population of Danzig was forcibly expelled, as were the *Volksdeutsche* or ethnic Germans of Kaliningrad, of

---

[178] Sadly appropriate that it should bear the name of another long-contested territory.
[179] His father was German, his mother Kashubian.

the Sudetenland in Czechoslovakia, of Danube Banovina[180] in Yugoslavia, and many other parts of Central and Eastern Europe whose historic German communities were brutally deported and even used as slave labour in the aftermath of the war. These *Heimatvertriebene* or expelled persons are still a force in German politics, and in their countries of origin, a taboo subject under communism and an unhealed wound.

But the role of Gdańsk in world history was not over by any means. In September 1980 an electrician at the Lenin Ship-yards started a movement that was to play a decisive role in the overthrow of the communist regime in Poland and ulti-mately the collapse of the entire Soviet bloc. He won the Nobel Peace Prize and was President of Poland from 1990 to 1995. His name was of course Lech Wałęsa and the union is Solidarność or Solidarity.

---

[180] The Banat region of the Serbian autonomous province of Vojvodina.

Skye

At the end of April 2007, it was widely reported that, by order of the Highland Council, the Isle of Skye had officially changed its name to Eilean a' Cheò. Skye was described as an 'anglicised slave name';[181] the change would help to 'promote the uniqueness of the Gaelic culture'. Some 40 per cent of Skye's 9,000-strong population speaks Gaelic, but presumably almost none of its 250,000 visitors a year. 'They won't have a clue where that is,' wailed a Skye bed-and-breakfast owner interviewed on Radio 4 (an incomer from the North of England who, despite living in the heart of the Gàidhealtachd,[182] knew neither the Gaelic name of the island nor even how to pronounce the word 'Gaelic' itself). 'It's just going to ruin the whole island I would think.'

Given that the supposed new name is commonly used neither in English nor Gaelic, it seems fair to assume that any such change would be of a rather theoretical sort. Eilean a' Cheò, a poetic nickname meaning 'isle of mists', is an interesting choice: doubtless pleasing to the romantic-minded visitor (the tourist trade is said to be worth £90 million a year), but not what Gaelic speakers actually call the place. The usual name is *an t-Eilean Sgitheanach*, often said to mean the Winged Isle, from the Gaelic *sgiath* ('wing') with reference to the shape of the island. However, this seems to be actually a reinterpretation of a pre-Celtic name. Ptolemy knew it as Sketis, though he mislocated it in his famous second-century

---

[181] A rather tasteless piece of hyperbole perhaps, coming so soon after the much-vaunted 200th anniversary of the abolition of the slave trade, as well as etymologically dubious.
[182] Gaelic-speaking area.

atlas; in St Adamnan's seventh-century *Life of Saint Columba* it turns up as Scia.

The name Dún Scáthaig, referring to a ruined castle once belonging to the barons of Sleat, comes from early tales that associate the island with the Irish mythological figure Scáthach, whose name means the shadowy one. She (yes, she) was a warrior who trained Cúchulainn, no less; she also invented and presented him with a kind of mystical harpoon called the *Gáe Bolg*.[183]

Names as various as Sligachan (Gaelic 'Place of Shells'), Pabay (Norse 'Priest Island') and Broadford (a literal English translation of the Gaelic *An t'ath Leathann*) speak of the mixed linguistic influence of Celts and Vikings on the island. Dunvegan, the ninth-century ancestral home of the MacLeods, seems to mean the 'Fort of the Few' (Gaelic *Dùn Bheagain*); a reference to a heroically defended early siege would be a suitably romantic derivation, though it may also be a Norse personal name, Began. It's the longest-continually inhabited house in Scotland, and home to clan relics such as Rory Mor's Horn, from which by tradition the heir must sink a bottle and a half of claret at a draught,[184] and the famous Fairy Flag, a large silk banner said to have been brought back from the Crusades (or was it the war standard of Harald Hardråde at the Battle of Stamford Bridge in 1066?) and to possess magic powers.[185]

Anyway, it turns out that the poor helpless tourists and the hysterical bed-and-breakfast owner[186] have nothing to worry about. The name Eilean a' Cheò refers only to the eleventh of the twenty-two Highland Council election wards, and we have

[183] He is sometimes said to have gained 'the friendship of her thighs', but one shouldn't listen to gossip.

[184] According to the guidebook this feat was performed in 1965 in 1 minute and 57 seconds.

[185] Members of the clan are even said to have carried photographs of it into battle with them during the Second World War.

[186] It was not stated which B-and-B she ran, but it would be fun if it was the one in Plockton called Nessun Dorma.

their word for it that 'there is no intention to change road signage or literature. The island will continue to be referred to as Skye.' Moral panic over then.

Herzegovina

This is one of those place names that carry a certain charge. Many of us remember Bosnia-Herzegovina as the scene of some of the worst atrocities of the Yugoslav wars of the 1990s, such as the mortar-bombing of civilians in the centre of Sarajevo on market day. At first the area was referred to as Bosnia-Herzegovina, but as time went on it generally seemed to be called Bosnia for simplicity. So where or what is this Herzegovina?

This, the most ethnically diverse region of Yugoslavia, was never going to be a simple matter to present on the evening news, and plenty of dumbing down was necessary. The way things were portrayed, there were the Serbs, who were Orthodox (appearing as the villains of the piece), the Croats, who were Catholics, and the Bosnians, who were Muslims; then there were the confusingly

named Bosnian Serbs, who lived in Bosnia but were Orthodox rather than Muslim,[187] and they, under their political figurehead Radovan Karadžić and their military strongman General Ratko Mladić, were the worst of all. Sarajevo, Srebrenica, Omarska, Bihać, Tuzla and Banya Luka – it can

[187] Rather like describing Ulster Protestants as Irish Scots.

seem as if there is hardly a Bosnian place name whose associations are not bloodstained.

The origin of the name Bosnia (Bosna to the locals) is not completely clear, but it has been around since classical times and probably comes from the River Bosna, or Bosanius. Herzegovina owes its name to the fact that that area was under the control of a Bosnian general called Stephen Vukčić Kosaăa, the first Serbian archbishop, who was made a duke by (probably) Pope Nicholas V. 'Duke' in Old Serbian is *herceg*, and Hercegovina, or Herzegovina as we more often spell it, simply means the lands of the duke. An older name is Zachumlje, after the Slavic *Zachlumoi* tribe, which strictly speaking refers to the area between Dubrovnik (formerly Ragusa) and the River Neretva, known in English as the Land of Hum[188] or Chelm.[189]

Balkans, specifically the area we know (or knew) as Yugoslavia, is a byword for political and ethnic complexity. The word 'balkanisation' entered the language in the early twentieth century to refer to the fracturing of a territory into small, often mutually hostile, units, as happened in the Balkans at the turn of the twentieth century and again in the 1990s. To consider another former Yugoslav republic famous for its ethnic diversity, the name Macedonia is often said to be the origin of the French culinary term *macédoine*, meaning a fruit salad or an assortment of vegetables, or more generally any 'medley or mixture of unrelated things'.[190]

Herzegovina lies on one of those fault lines between old empires. For some four centuries it was ruled by the Turks as

[188] There is still a place called Hum (which simply means 'hill') in the northwest corner of Croatia, named by the *Guinness Book of Records* as the world's smallest town. It has 17 inhabitants.

[189] Not to be confused with Chelm, the town in Poland which is the symbol of stupidity in Jewish humour, or the not-even-slightly-funny Chełmno near Łódź which was the site of a Nazi death camp.

[190] It's just a theory, however: the spoilsport word-drudges of Oxford warn that 'the suggestion that it refers to the diversity of peoples in the Macedonian empire of Alexander the Great has not been fully established'.

part of the Ottoman Empire (which is of course why there are more Muslims there than in, say, Slovenia), then by the Austro-Hungarian Empire from 1878 to 1918. It was annexed by the Nazis and ceded to their puppet state in Croatia, where under the fascist Ustaše not only the significant Jewish and Gypsy communities were persecuted and murdered, but also the 750,000 or so Croatian Serbs.

These are indeed tiny areas we're talking about. Herzegovina is about half the size of Wales.[191] The larger units from which these smaller states emerged were of course the mighty empires that ruled Europe before the rise of the nation state, and after that of Yugoslavia, the confederation of southern Slavs that fell apart so bloodily at the end of the Soviet era. Thus, as so often, the borders of principalities and powers ebb and flow turbulently around ordinary mortals; and, never more tragically than here, bullets and mortars fly too.

[191] Wales is of course the traditional rule-of-thumb unit of geographical area for British purposes. Apparently the Americans often measure using the tiny state of Delaware, 'Uncle Sam's Pocket Handkerchief' – about one eighth of the size of Wales if that helps you picture it. That must seem very small indeed in a country where mighty Texas weighs in at about 280 Delawares, which is 35 Waleses – and as we all know, Texas is not even the largest United State, not by a long way.

San Serriffe

This exotic island group is surely one of the world's great mysteries. No record of it appears in the massive *Times Comprehensive Atlas of the World*, nor yet the *Times Atlas of World History*, the *Times Atlas of World Exploration* or the *Dorling Kindersley World Reference Atlas*, and it is unknown to the *Encyclopaedia Britannica, Funk & Wagnalls* and *Encarta*. As for the august Oxford University Press, neither its *World Encyclopaedia* nor its *Concise Dictionary of World Place-Names* has heard of such a place, and even Google Earth cannot seem to find it. The *CIA World Factbook* has nothing to say – or perhaps its lips are sealed?

San Serriffe is an archipelago consisting of two main islands, Caissa Superiore and Caissa Inferiore. Caissa Superiore (Upper Caisse) is roughly circular. Just to the south lies Caissa Inferiore (Lower Caisse) with its southwestern promontory, shaped something like a comma. The dominant ethnic group are the Colons, descendants of the first European settlers, who are ethnic Italics, and there is also a large mixed-race population known as Semicolons. Forty years ago power was seized by a bold character called General Pica, who imposed a very heavy type of repressive regime, and changed the name of the country to Picador.

And yet this place seems to have escaped the attention of the outside world until just thirty years ago, when the *Guardian* newspaper published an in-depth report about it, right at the beginning of April. Indeed, some have gone so far as to cast doubt on its very existence.

Tanganyika

Whatever happened to Tanganyika? Well, it's still there. Unlike some African countries, Tanganyika is largely defined by natural borders. To the east is the Indian Ocean, to the northwest lies Lake Victoria, and the River Ruvuma supplies the southern frontier. The border with Kenya may be an artificially straight line, skirting just north of Mount Kilimanjaro,[192] but the western boundary is one of the most spectacular geographical features of Africa: the Great Rift Valley, and along it the two mighty lakes Malawi (formerly Nyasa) and Tanganyika.

Although Germany was not in the same league as Britain and France when it came to carving out an African empire, it did have some foreign colonies, and in 1884 Tanganyika was annexed into German East Africa. The territory to the south, now Mozambique, was ruled by the Portuguese, but on all other sides Tanganyika was surrounded by British territory, famously coloured pink on imperial-era maps. In the First World War Tanganyika was captured by the British; it was mandated to the League of Nations in 1922 and thereafter made a trust territory of the United Nations.

Just across the water lies Zanzibar, part of what was sometimes called the Spice Islands after its production of such precious commodities as nutmeg, cloves, cinnamon and pepper. Originally colonised by Persians, it had been a Portuguese possession from 1503 to 1698, and a British protectorate since 1890 – not to mention being the birthplace of Freddie Mercury in 1946. Tanganyika gained independence in 1961, and three years later merged with the newly

[192] And why is that? See British Heligoland on page 32.

independent Zanzibar, whose Sultan had just been toppled in a coup, to became Tanzania – a blend of the names Tanganyika and Zanzibar.

Its post-colonial experience has been happier than that of many of its neighbours; Julius Nyerere[193] was unusual among leaders of African one-party states, not only in sporting an incongruous Hitler moustache, but in retiring of his own free will when his economic policies had had their day. Untainted by scandal, he was largely revered as an elder statesman until his death in 1999. Meanwhile, with such natural wonders as Mount Kilimanjaro, the Ngorongoro Crater, the Serengeti National Park and two of Africa's great lakes falling inside its borders, not to mention substantial reserves of gold and gas, Tanzania surely has plenty going for it.

On the coast just to the south of Zanzibar is the old port of Dar es Salaam ('safe port'), through which not only spices but human cargoes were traded, and this was the capital until very recently.[194] The nickname of Dar es Salaam is 'Bongo' or 'Bongoland', from the Swahili for 'brain', no doubt referring to the fact that the best way to get ahead in the big

---

[193] Nyerere was sometimes known as *Mwalimu*, 'teacher', and claimed to be 'a schoolmaster by choice and a politician by accident'. The first Tanzanian to go to a British university (Edinburgh), he translated Shakespeare into Swahili and enjoyed bookbinding and Mateus rosé. Not quite our image of the decadent despot who takes the presidential jet to Paris every month for a haircut.

[194] It has now moved to Dodoma, at least in theory.

city is to be streetwise and use your head. So Tanganyika can perhaps make a case for being the original 'Bongo-Bongo Land', that blimpish term sometimes used to refer dismissively to undeveloped Third World countries.

Even more dismissive is Captain Edmund Blackadder's jocular analysis in *Blackadder Goes Forth*, set during the First World War: 'The British Empire at present covers a quarter of the globe, while the German Empire consists of a small sausage factory in Tanganyika. I hardly think that we can be entirely absolved of blame on the imperialistic front.' Jocular, but not without a grain of truth. It's often the way.[195]

---

[195] At least, we hope you'll think so.

Index

Index of People

Index of Places